TREACHERY

Also by Michael E Wills

Finn's Fate
Three Kings – One Throne
The Wessex Turncoat
One Decent Thing
A TEFLER's Tale
Children of the Chieftain: Betrayed
Children of the Chieftain: Banished
Children of the Chieftain: Bounty
Children of the Chieftain: Bound for Home
Sven and the Purse of Silver
The Red Slipper
Izar, The Amesbury Archer
Treason : A Story of Children Evacuated in 1940

TREACHERY

A second story of children evacuated in 1940

MICHAEL E WILLS

Published in 2022 by Michael E Wills

Copyright © Michael E Wills 2022

The right of Michael E Wills to be identified as the author of this work has been asserted in accordance with the Copyright, Designs and Patents Act 1988 Sections 77 and 78.

This book is a work of fiction and while places mentioned in the book are based on fact, any similarity between characters appearing in the story and actual figures, alive or dead, is entirely coincidental.

ISBN 978-1-7398588-1-0

CONTENTS

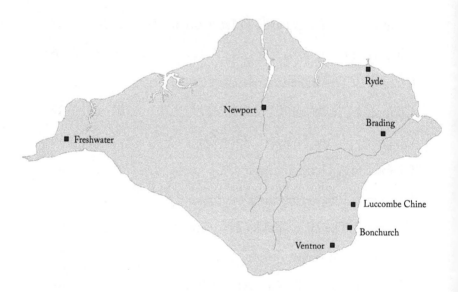

The Isle of Wight

CHAPTER 1

Cliff Top Farm - 21st February 1941

"Half-term holiday at last!" shouted Jimmy as he came through the front door, followed by the others. He shrugged off his school satchel and hung it up on one of the pegs on the back of the door.

"Not there, Jimmy. Take it to your room, please," said his mother.

Judith and Alfie took the hint and did not copy Jimmy's example, but rather took their bags with them as they went upstairs to change out of their school uniforms.

"All come down as soon as you can, you each have jobs to do before it gets dark," called Vera.

The children knew the evening routine well. Alfie tended to the geese and collected the hens' eggs laid during the day, Judith looked after the horses, and Jimmy fed the pigs. Soon Vera heard the thumping sound of them running down the stairs.

From the kitchen, the unmistakable smell of frying onions permeated the air.

"What's for supper, Mum?" asked Jimmy as he put on his boots.

"Something special today, I managed to get some sausages from the butcher. I had to queue for half an hour. Shopping is getting more and more difficult. They say that cheese is to be rationed from next month, tea as well."

"What else?"

"Potato cakes with onion and boiled cabbage."

"Not cabbage again!"

"Yes, and I expect you to set a good example to Alfie and eat all of yours."

Jimmy let out a groan as he picked up the swill bucket. Each evening he mixed up the food leftovers with corn, raw potatoes, and cabbage, and shared it between the expectant sows. When he had finished his chores, he and Alfie listened to *Children's Hour* on his wireless. Judith preferred to spend her time reading the latest book she had got from the school library.

At six o'clock, Vera shouted up the stairs, "Supper's ready. Table layers required!"

It was over supper each evening that the children reported on their day at school and generally chatted about life on the farm, but on Fridays they also made plans for the weekend.

"This is a special Friday, no school for a week," said Vera.

"We can sleep late for seven days!"

"Oh no you can't, Jimmy. Your daily chores have to be done as usual. The animals are not on holiday, and they wake at the same time."

"Can we go riding?" asked Judith.

8

"Yes, I'm sure we can find time to exercise the horses. However, I have a bit of news."

"What news?"

"Well, Judith, first of all, let me say that I think you are all doing very well and working like a real farming team. In particular, you and Alfie, as children who were brought up in cities and are now evacuees, have adapted to country life. Even though Alfie is the youngest, he really contributes to making the farm run smoothly. Jimmy had the advantage of growing up here, but he has had to adapt too. After all, last September he suddenly got a younger brother and sister his own age."

"So, what's the news?" asked Jimmy.

Vera took a deep breath; she knew that what she was going to say would not be popular.

TRUE FACTS!

Rationing came in gradually during the Second World War. The first thing to be rationed, in 1939, was petrol and diesel. In 1940 food began to be rationed: this included meat (to the value of 6p per week), butter (50g), sugar (225g), tea (50g), and cooking fat (100g). In 1941, eggs, cheese, and jam were included. By 1942, almost all food was rationed.

Each shopper had to present their ration books, which listed their allowances. The shop keeper crossed off each item from the list as it was bought.

"The Ministry of Food has told some farmers, including us, to change from growing wheat to growing potatoes."

There was a groan from Jimmy.

"Why, ain't the wheat no good?" asked Alfie.

"No, it's not that. It is because there is a shortage of potatoes, and the soil around here is very good for growing them. You'll see, at Churchfield Farm next to our land, they will be doing the same."

"Will it make any difference to what we have to do?"

"Yes, I can tell from Jimmy's groan that he has realised what it is. It means that there will be more work for us to do. We plant wheat using a seed drill on the tractor, but potatoes have to be planted by hand. Hundreds and hundreds of them."

"Oh, I see. When must they be planted?" asked Judith.

"By the end of February," replied Vera.

"But next week is the last week in February."

"Yes, Judith, so I am afraid my farming team has got a lot of extra work to do during their half term holiday."

"Can't we get some more help?" moaned Jimmy.

"Since we lost our farm hand last year, it has been impossible to get a replacement. All the men are in the armed forces. But I have asked the County Council to see if they can find someone, perhaps a man who is too old for army service."

"When will we start?" asked Judith.

"On Monday. Tomorrow the Ministry of Food is delivering sacks of seed potatoes for us to plant."

"How do we do it?"

"Well, Alfie, I drive the tractor with a two-blade plough in very straight lines across the field. That makes two deep lines, furrows. You come along behind and put potatoes into the furrows. Then when you have finished, I come back with the tractor and cover over the potatoes."

"It sounds easy, Mum," said Judith.

Jimmy laughed and said, "Easy yes, but very tiring."

"Right, so we start on Monday morning. I do have some good news for you. I took a few eggs to town and the grocer swapped them for a bag of sweets he had behind the counter.

The present ration for eggs is one per week for adults, so we are very lucky to have our own supply."

"What do you mean 'behind the counter'?" asked Judith.

Vera was silent for a moment and then Jimmy said, "Tell her, Mum."

"Well, you see, Judith, sometimes the grocer has more of some things than customers have ration allowance for. So, he keeps them behind the counter to swap for things he can't get."

"Such as eggs!" exclaimed Judith.

"Yes, dear. That is how it works. Now, off to bed, all of you."

Jimmy was on his bed, reading by the light of the oil lamp, when he heard the sound of a car coming down the farm track. He pulled back the black-out blind and saw the dim lights of a vehicle stopping outside the farmhouse. Shortly after, he heard the thump of someone knocking at the front door. Inquisitive as ever, he quietly crept to the top of the stairs to look and listen.

His mother had opened the front door and let two men in. One he recognised. The other, a stranger in a very smart uniform with well-polished buttons and a leather strap across his chest, was obviously an army officer.

"Good evening, Mr Stevens. To what do I owe the pleasure of this late evening visit?"

"Good evening, Mrs Orton. May I introduce to you Captain Morley."

The captain nodded to Vera and said, "Good evening, Mrs Orton. I apologise for the lateness of our visit, but the matter is urgent."

Vera said, "Excuse me a moment."

She walked across the room to the bottom of the stairs and just caught sight of the figure at the top as he sought to hide.

"Jimmy, I guessed you would be there. Off to bed with you."

She turned and said, "Gentlemen, do sit down."

When the three of them were sitting at the kitchen table, she said, "Well, gentlemen, what is this urgent matter?"

Mr Stevens cleared his throat and began.

"Although it is not strictly my department, it has been brought to my attention that you have sought help from the County Council to obtain manual assistance in matters pertaining to the running of your farm."

"Yes, if you mean that I have asked for a farm hand, that is so."

"As you are aware, all men of an eligible age have been conscripted into the armed forces or have reserved occupations that prevent them from serving."

"Yes."

"We are unable to help you with your request. However, the government has seen fit to allow some incarcerated individuals, that is, prisoners, to work on farms. Captain Morley will explain."

> **TRUE FACTS!**
>
> By 1943, there were 76,000 Italian prisoners in the UK and this rose to 158,000 in 1945. Almost half of the prisoners agreed to work; they were called co-operators. Prisoners were given a packet of cigarettes a week and paid 5 pence (2p in today's money) a day. Those who chose to work could earn more and be allowed to spend it in special mobile shops. They had to have a red patch sewn on to their clothes to identify them as prisoners of war (POW).

"Mrs Orton, since the army's successful campaign in defending Egypt, a large number of Italian soldiers have surrendered. Many of these have been transported to England and are living in prisoner of war camps. The government, recognising the shortage of manpower in agriculture, has encouraged prisoners to volunteer to work on farms within a five-mile radius of their prison camp. Those that volunteer get certain privileges that others do not."

"So how does this affect me?" asked Vera.

Captain Morley continued, "The army has requisitioned, that is to say, taken over ownership, of the cottage and the previous guest house that adjoins your farm. Thirty Italian prisoners will be living there. Roughly half of them have volunteered to do farm work. These will be shared out between farms in the district. Your allocation, if you accept, will be an officer and three privates."

"Aren't they dangerous? They are the enemy after all."

"We find that those who volunteer are generally cooperative and decent men who are just pleased to be out harm's way in North Africa. However, just to be careful, two of my men, armed with rifles and fixed bayonets, will accompany the Italians at all times."

The officer seemed to have completed his speech. There was silence for a while and then Mr Stevens spoke.

"So, there you have it, Mrs Orton. How do you feel about the proposal?"

"What will I have to pay for these men?"

Captain Morley quickly said, "The volunteers are paid an allowance by the government, there is no cost to you. However, you are expected to provide them with a simple lunch on some days."

"For which you will be allowed extra rations," intervened Mr Stevens.

"Then I agree. When can they start?"

"Would Monday suit you?" asked the captain.

"Monday would suit me very well indeed."

As the two men stood up to leave, Vera said, "Oh, Mr Stevens, could I have a word in private? And, Captain Morley, I forgot to ask, will the Italians understand English?"

"Doubtful, but the officer probably will, and he can translate."

The captain made a diplomatic exit, leaving Mr Stevens alone with Vera.

"Mr Stevens, you may remember that when I agreed to take a second evacuee child, I made a condition."

"Er, um, oh dear, it had completely slipped my mind."

"The condition was an extra ration of diesel for my tractor in recognition of the fact that I have more journeys to make ferrying the children to and from school."

"Oh, yes, I um, ten gallons a month, wasn't it?"

"Yes, it was. Now if I don't get that fuel, I will not be able to run my farm and ferry children hither and thither."

"I can assure you I will attend to it. I am extremely sorry to have overlooked this. Please accept my apologies."

"I will accept your apologies on yet another condition."

Very hesitantly, Mr Stevens said, "Yes, what have you in mind?"

"Alfie Field, the boy I agreed to take, in addition to the girl, came to the Island with his younger sister, Pauline. When they got off the ferry, the pair were split up and she went on a different train from him. I would like you to find which family she was placed with and make arrangements for her to visit her brother during the half-term holiday."

"Mrs Orton, I really don't think that this is my responsibility."

"Mr Stevens, you let me down on an agreement. This has caused me considerable anxiety and inconvenience. I think that the least you could do is to make amends."

"Yes, I, I see your point, Mrs Orton. I'll see what I can do."

"Thank you, Mr Stevens. I think we understand each other."

"Yes, indeed. Good night to you, Mrs Orton."

Vera smiled to herself as she closed the front door and pushed the bolt across.

CHAPTER 2

A Pig for a Car

On Saturday morning the children were once more involved in their least favourite occupation: cleaning the house. Any excuse to pause in their work was welcome, but the sight and sound of an old van lumbering up the drive to the farmhouse, followed by a slightly dilapidated red and black car, warranted a complete stop of work and a gathering at the front of the building. However, when Vera emerged from the kitchen, she quickly tried to shoo the workers back to their tasks.

"Come on, everyone, you have work to do. I need to have a private conversation with our visitors."

Begrudgingly, Jimmy returned to the carpet hanging on the line and resumed beating it. Judith went back to the sweeping indoors and Alfie made off in the direction of the stable to get clean straw for the goose pen.

The door of the van creaked open and a man of medium height, wearing a grey suit, which had seen better days, stepped out. As he turned towards Vera, he lifted his trilby hat, revealing black hair that was brushed back and plastered to his head by some kind of hair cream. He had a short, well-trimmed moustache and his smile betrayed a gold front tooth. Looking across at him, Jimmy could see that the man's shoes were polished, but they were quite inappropriate for walking around a farmyard. All attention was on the man and no one noticed the occupant of the car as he furtively crept off in a different direction.

"Mrs Orton, it's a pleasure to meet you. Joe Chivers at your service."

"Good morning, Mr Chivers. I understand from your letter that you have a business proposition for me.."

"Indeed I do, good lady. I had heard rumours around Ventnor that um, how shall put it? That your fine brood of children use a method of transport to school which, on wet winter days, exposes them to the ravages of the weather. Thus, there is a risk that the less hardy among them might easily succumb to illness, to colds, flu or worse."

"Mr Chivers, would you come to the point!"

"Yes, of course, Mrs Orton. By profession, I am a trader. A man of the highest repute. I assist people in obtaining that which they desire. I have not acquired the nickname of 'honest Joe' by anything less than providing satisfaction to all those I have dealings with."

Before Vera could respond there was a loud shout from the direction of the hens' coup. It was clearly identifiable as Alfie's voice. The two adults turned towards the direction of the sound but their view was obscured by the farm building. However, a few seconds later they saw a young man racing out from around the corner of the coup pursued by an angry goose. The goose in turn was being followed by Alfie.

"He were stealing eggs, Mum! Pinching them from the nesting box!"

"Did he take any?" called Vera.

"No, I let the gander out of the pen."

Vera, though indignant about the attempted theft, could not but laugh as she said, "Honest Joe, who is your dishonest companion?"

"Ma'am, I done my best to bring that lad up. I really try to teach him to follow the straight and narrow, but it is hard with young people these days. I blame Mrs Chivers, she's too soft with him."

"I hope he is not taking his example from you, Mr Chivers. I have to say that his behaviour gives me no confidence in you."

"But, Mrs Orton, I do apologise most profusely. I can assure you that you can trust me utterly. By way of restoring your confidence, let me offer you a small gift."

He turned and, gingerly avoiding the muddy pools on the path, opened his van door and lifted something from the passenger seat. When he came back, he was carrying a package that was quite clearly a bag of sugar.

"Please take this as a small gift, Mrs Orton."

She looked at the bag and said, "I won't ask where you got it."

"Indeed, you can, dear lady, the truth is, I was following a lorry and some bags of sugar fell off the back. I really tried to catch up with the lorry to tell the driver, but my van was not fast enough."

Vera took the bag and said, "Shall we resume our discussion? I guess from your comments that you want to sell me a car."

"That is most perceptive of you, madam. The truth is, a dear old lady, a distant relative of mine, is recently deceased. May she rest in peace."

"And she no longer needs the car," said Vera.

"That, in a nutshell, is my dilemma. I have a car I don't need. It is, thus, for sale."

"Mr Chivers, I am afraid to disappoint you. You see, while I do indeed need a car, I lack the money to buy even the cheapest."

"Ah, Mrs Orton, you are talking to the right man! My motto is, "Never let the lack of cash get in the way of a good deal."

"Tell me more."

"The fine vehicle parked there behind my van is a 1929 Austin 7 Saloon with four seats. The body is aluminium so there is no rust. Come and inspect it."

Mr Chivers ushered Vera round the back of his van and regaled her with all the virtues of the car.

"Get out, Jack," he said to the thwarted egg thief. "Try the driving seat, Mrs Orton."

Vera climbed into the small vehicle while the trader continued to gush praise for the car. At length, she got out.

"So, what are you proposing that I should use in the place of money, Mr Chivers?"

"Mrs Orton, I know that you are going to think that I am stupid, that I am going to be the loser in this deal I am about to propose, but it reflects the respect that I feel for those like you, who labour night and day to ensure that the embattled people of this great country have enough to eat. You are going to think me a poor businessman to offer you a deal so very obviously in your favour at a cost to me."

19

"Mr Chivers, would you please, please get to the point?"

"The point, yes, the point is I have a client, a gentleman farmer. A very well-spoken gent…"

"Come to the point, Mr Chivers!"

"Of course, this highly respectable man would like to go into pig farming. He needs an expectant sow."

"I see. So, you are offering the car in return for a sow?"

"Yes, indeed, madam."

"What proof do you have that you actually own the car?"

"Mrs Orton, surely you do not suspect me of dishonesty?"

"Not at all, Mr Chivers, but it makes good sense. I can prove that I own the sow, can you prove you own the car?"

"Indeed, I can."

He delved into his inside pocket and withdrew a shabby document.

"Here is the logbook. See, there is my name."

Vera looked at the document and then said, "Excuse me a moment. I have to consult my son."

Her conversation with Jimmy was short, though he was puzzled by the fact that a sow could be worth a car. Vera explained to him, "These days, with limited fuel supply and petrol on strict ration, no one wants to buy a car, so they are not worth very much."

The deal being agreed, the next problem was for Mr Chivers and Jack to get the sow into the van, a procedure both noisy and dirty, but which provided great entertainment for the children.

When they had eventually gone, Vera said, "Well, children, when you go back to school in a week's time, you will be doing so in the warm and dry and not on the back of the tractor trailer!"

"What are we going to call the car?" asked Jimmy.

"Tim" said Judith.

"Why Tim?" asked Jimmy

"Well, it's tiny and in Dickens's book, *A Christmas Carol*, Tim is called Tiny Tim."

"That sounds a good explanation!" exclaimed Vera. "So, Tim it is."

CHAPTER 3

The Italians Arrive

Vera realised that a wet Sunday yesterday would mean a muddy Monday today, not the best conditions for the potato planting. Jimmy was well aware of this too.

"Don't say anything to the others, Jimmy, we don't want to dishearten them."

"Good thing you got the new tyres for the tractor, the ground is going to be very heavy," he replied.

"Yes, but the potatoes have got to go in, so we'll get started straight after breakfast. Oh, good morning, Judith, come and sit down. Have you seen Alfie?"

"Good morning, he's just coming. What's for breakfast?"

"A poor woman's breakfast today I'm afraid, milk sop."

"Oh, Mum, you really must get to the grocer's today," protested Jimmy.

"No time today I'm afraid," she said as she poured hot milk over the slice of bread in Judith's bowl.

"Thanks, Mum. I quite like milk sop."

"It all right I suppose, as long as we can spare a little sugar to go on it. Tomorrow we'll have a treat and use some of the eggs. Ah, Alfie, good morning."

"Mornin', Mum," said the boy.

"I was just saying that we'll use some of the eggs you've been saving and have a special breakfast tomorrow."

Alfie smiled and sat down.

"Now, as you know, we have a big job today, in fact it will take us several days."

Vera stopped for a moment, anticipating that there might be some groans. There were none.

She continued, "I took the potato seed sacks down to the field yesterday. You will each have a bucket. You fill it with potatoes from the sacks and then do as I described before. Jimmy will show you how far apart you should plant the seed."

Alfie asked the question they all wanted to, "Must we do it all day, Mum?"

TRUE FACTS

When there were no more food coupons in the ration book or money ran short, mothers had to be inventive with food.

Milk sop – slices of bread soaked in milk and, if available, a sprinkle of sugar on top.

Fairy Toast – wafer thin slices of stale bread baked in an oven until golden brown and used in place of biscuits or bread.

Toad in the hole – a sausage or two, baked in batter and served with gravy.

Bread and Dripping – the left-over animal fat from beef or pork is allowed to cool and is then spread on slices of bread. It is served with a sprinkle of salt on top.

"Yes, I'm afraid so, but we'll stop for a drink and a biscuit during the morning and then come back here for some lunch."

"What about if it rains?" asked Alfie.

"It depends how heavy it is. However, I do have some good news for you."

All the children suddenly looked a lot more alert.

"What's that, Mum?" asked Jimmy.

"You've seen the army lorries driving up the road at the end of our lane. They have transferred some Italian prisoners of war to the old guest house. They are going to live there until a proper prison camp has been built for them."

"Won't they just run away from there?" asked Jimmy.

Vera laughed. "Where could they run to? This is an island and besides, there are army guards to keep a watch on them."

"How did they get caught?" asked Alfie.

Vera had to answer a number of questions about how the prisoners came to be on the Island, as best she could, before Jimmy said, "How is this good news for us?"

"Ah, I was coming to that. Some of the prisoners have volunteered to work on our farm. Four of them will be joining us this morning to help with the potato planting."

There was a silence.

"Aren't you glad that you are going to get some help?"

"But they might be dangerous, they are the enemy, aren't they?" asked Jimmy.

Vera laughed again.

"These men have probably had enough of danger and war; they are most likely just normal people who happen to live in a country with different opinions to ours."

"How do you know they won't hurt us?" asked Judith. She was still very upset about bombing in London, which had destroyed her home, and she seemed the most hesitant of the children about the prospect of enemy soldiers being nearby.

"I forgot to tell you. There will be two English soldiers coming with them and the soldiers will have guns. So, the prisoners would not in any case be a threat to us and we really could do with the extra help. We'll do the job in half the time. Ah, that reminds me of a quiz question."

"Go on, tell us," said Judith.

"If you know the answer, whisper it to me after breakfast, don't tell anyone else. So here it is: There was a farmer who had to plant potatoes in his field. He asked his neighbours to come to help him. Each day, more of them came, so every day they planted double the number they had planted the day before. On the eighth day, they finished the whole field. My question is, "On which day had they planted half the field?""

This puzzle seemed to allay much of the children's concern, though none of them rushed to whisper in Vera's ear. They finished breakfast and then did their normal morning chores before assembling in front of the house with their buckets.

"Look, here they come!" shouted Jimmy, pointing to the end of the lane.

A soldier with a rifle slung over his shoulder was holding the gate open for four men and another soldier. The group then formed up in twos, with the soldiers at the back, and marched towards the house.

As they approached Vera and the children, it was obvious that the Italians were still wearing their army uniforms, although in most cases they were somewhat tattered and torn. Each of them had a red arm band sewn onto their sleeve.

Despite their situation, the men were grinning and making comments to each other.

One of the English soldiers moved to the front of the group and turned to the others.

"All right, you lot, shut up."

The soldier, who had two stripes on his uniform sleeve, turned back to face Vera and in a loud voice said, "Morning, Ma'am. Corporal Trent commanding prisoner detail and Private Jenkins, at your service."

"Good morning, Corporal. Good to see you. Jimmy, stop Billy growling."

"Sorry about the dog, he is wary of strangers."

The soldier paid no attention to the animal and continued.

"May I see your husband, Ma'am, to make arrangements for the work?"

The children were amused when Vera said, "I no longer have a husband, I am the farmer."

The soldier's confidence was somewhat shaken as he considered his next question.

"Then, Ma'am, will you be the employer?" he asked hesitantly.

One of the Italians, a slightly tubby man with a finely trimmed moustache, who had a somewhat smarter appearance than the rest, had obviously understood what was being said, for he turned to the others and translated. They started making comments between themselves.

The corporal turned and shouted at the men, "Hold your gabble, you lot! Major, tell them to shut up."

It was clear that the Italian major was the translator.

When the soldier turned back to face her, Vera said, "Yes, Corporal, I will be the employer, so let's get to work. Ask the major to translate what I have to say, please."

"Yes, Ma'am."

The major stepped forward and bowed to Vera. From her side, Billy started to growl. The prisoner held his forefinger to his lips and the dog immediately calmed down.

"I am Major Luigi Balzarini of Bologna, Italy. My profession before the army was that of a policeman detective. An officer of some rank. I now have the misfortune to be a prisoner, but the honour to be at your service, Madam."

"It's a pleasure to meet you, Luigi, my name is Vera Orton. Do please call me Vera. I see you have a way with dogs."

"Thank you, Signora[1] Vera, it is one of my, er.. what do you say, er.. several talents. I have very well-trained dogs of my own." Looking at the young ones, he added, "If I may remark, what fine children you have."

He turned to the other three men and, pointing at the children, shouted, "Bei ragazzi!"[2]

There was a chorus in Italian of what seemed to be agreement.

Vera quickly decided that now was not the time to go into explanations about who the children were. She nodded her head and just said, "Thank you".

The corporal said nothing, but it was clear to Vera that he did not approve of such familiarity with the prisoners.

"But, Signora, you must excuse me, my current state of confinement as a prisoner is no reason for lack of civility. May

---

1   Signora = Mrs

2   Bei Ragazzi = Fine children

I introduce my men to you, for they do not have the education to introduce themselves."

"Come on, come on, Major, we're here to work," interrupted the corporal brusquely.

"I beg for just one moment, Corporal. The man who is tallest, he is Private Salvatore Bruschi. Before joining the army, he was an engineer. The man with the bird, who is from the very south of my country, is Carlo Sigismondi, a farmer."

The major stopped, conscious of some giggling around him.

"Major, I think you mean 'beard', not 'bird,' said Vera.

"Ah, Signora, I crave your pardon. And the tiniest man is Giuseppe Locarno. He is also the loudest man, for his work is opera singer."

"Right, that's it, now let's hear what Mrs Orton has to say," said Corporal Trent fiercely.

Vera then briefed the men about what was expected of them. While she was doing so the children stood watching and listening. Alfie and Jimmy were most interested in the soldiers' rifles, while Judith was fascinated to hear the translation of Vera's instructions. She recognised some words through her knowledge of French and the little Italian she had learnt when she holidayed in Italy with her parents. Looking at the men, she felt somewhat reassured. They looked just like normal people, though all of them had black hair and the farmer really did have a very thick beard. Such of his face that could be seen had a very swarthy complexion, which made him look somewhat villainous.

"Children, give the men your buckets and go to the stable to get some more for yourselves. Luigi, wait for them to come back. My son, Jimmy, will show you and your men the way to the field. I'll go ahead with the tractor."

The soldiers and the prisoners stared wide-eyed as Vera deftly mounted the tractor, started the engine and then very accurately backed it out of the gap between the house and the pig pens before driving off towards their place of work. As she passed the group of people she stopped and shouted to the corporal, "What will the men do about lunch?"

"Don't worry, Ma'am, today they have sandwiches with them," he replied, pointing at the haversack the man in front of him was carrying on a strap over his shoulder.

By the time the men and the children reached the field, Vera was some distance away, leaving two long furrows behind the tractor. The men stood still, looking at the muddy mess in front of them. Luigi shouted something to the other three, and they started work.

Though they chattered a lot and, occasionally, Giuseppe's fine tenor voice filled the air with snippets of opera music, which the others joined in with, the men soon got into the swing of the work and progress was quickly evident.

Meanwhile the major stood on the edge of the field watching.

"Come on, Major, get on with it!" demanded the corporal.

"But, Corporal, you cannot seriously expect a man of my rank to work in these circumstances."

"You volunteered like the others. You have to work as well."

"No, I volunteered the men under my command. See how well they are working! I must stay watching, to give orders."

The exasperated corporal stepped over to consult the private. They both walked to where they were out of the major's earshot.

"He has a point, Corporal. These blokes will work better if they have an officer who speaks their lingo to keep an eye on them."

"But he can't just hang around here doing no real work. He gets extra pay for this."

"Well, we need him to translate, you can't do without him."

"That's true. I'll ask the missus if there's some other job here for his lordship where he won't get muddy hands."

It was not until their mid-morning break that Vera stopped the tractor and the children gathered around her.

"Well done, it's going very well. Jimmy, there is a flask of milk and some biscuits in the bag behind the tractor driver's seat."

"What are we going to drink out of?" asked Judith.

"Ah, sorry, I forgot the glasses. Judith, you drink out of the flask first and then pass it to the others."

"The Italians have stopped work for a break, but they haven't got anything to drink," observed Jimmy.

"Um…not planned very well, is it."

As she spoke, the corporal was walking towards her.

"Corporal, these men, and you too I expect, would like a drink."

"Well, the major keeps moaning about having no coffee."

Vera laughed. "We haven't seen coffee since 1939. I have some tea, though. I'm too busy, one of the men would have to make a pot for them."

"I have just the man to do it!"

"Who?"

"Major!" he shouted.

The major sauntered over to the group.

"Yes, Corporal. How can I give you assistance?"

"You clearly have the interests of your men at heart. We would like you to make some tea for them."

The major was about to protest when he realised that an indoor job, albeit for only part of the day, would be preferable to the risk of being forced to work in the mud.

"Certainly, Corporal."

"Jimmy, you take Luigi to the house and show him where things are," said Vera.

"Pardon me, Ma'am, but I have to insist that Private Jenkins accompanies them."

"Oh yes, of course, Corporal. I forgot that we are still at war," said Vera jokingly.

"Come on, the rest of you, back to work. You can have a break when the major gets back."

The three of them all looked at their commander questioningly, and he explained in Italian. There were some gesticulations and shouts, which seemed to be of approval.

"Oh and, Jimmy, bring some of my home-made biscuits."

CHAPTER 4

An Italian Cook

"Come in, Major, I'll show you where the kitchen is," said Jimmy.

The officer entered the house, followed by Private Jenkins, who took his rifle off his shoulder so that the bayonet did not scrape the door frame.

"Here's the kitchen."

"Mamma Mia! This is just like the kitchen of my grandmother. She was a farmer too."

Jimmy was not sure if this was a complement or a criticism. He answered politely, "Really, what did she grow?."

"Olives, but she kept goats too."

Private Jenkins had no patience for small talk and interrupted. "Where's the stuff for making tea then?"

Jimmy passed the kettle to Luigi and said, "You will need to stoke up the fire and boil water in this. There's the tea pot, the tea is in that tin. There's milk in a jug in the larder over there."

The major was scanning various food items that were arrayed on shelves.

"Tell me, young Jimmy, do you have flour?"

"Yes, in the tin over there."

"And eggs?"

"Well yes, but we are very careful about using them because they're on ration."

Jimmy was careful not to betray the fact that they used their excess eggs to barter for other things at the grocers.

"Why, what's this got to do with you, Major?" demanded the private in an irritated voice.

"It is just a thought I had, Private, just a thought."

"I must get back to the field," said Jimmy.

He left the two men in the kitchen and made his way back to work.

It was while the potato planters were having their lunch break that the major approached Vera.

"Signora Vera, my men appreciate that they have food for their lunch. But it is, how shall I say, it is difficult for them to like these, what do you call them, er…sandwiches."

He pointed to the three men. They were peeling the top layer of bread off their thick sandwiches and peering inside to identify the contents.

"Then they will have to accustomise themselves to English food, Major," said Vera.

The corporal had overheard the conversation and added, "And be grateful that we feed them at all!"

The major was not abashed by the comment and continued in a sly voice.

"One of my many achievements is to be an excellent cook. Men are the best cooks in my country. Would you allow me to use your delightful kitchen to prepare a lunch dish for all, tomorrow?"

"For everyone?"

"Yes, the ragazzi[3], the soldiers and, of course, for you, Signora."

"We don't want no foreign grub. We got good English sandwiches, though not enough of 'em," growled the corporal.

"But, Corporal, I have an easy solution for you. If the lovely Signora Vera will allow me to prepare this dish, one which is the most typical and traditional of my region, then you and Private Jenkins could have the sandwiches of my men."

This argument threw the corporal. He was silent for a moment while he considered the idea.

"Sounds all right to me, Corp!" said the private, who had overheard the conversation.

"Wait a minute, all of you," said Vera. "We have strict food rationing, I can't be expected to provide food for the prisoners to have an Italian banquet."

"Most understandably so, Signora, but the ingredients I need are few, and I have seen that you have them."

"What are they?"

"Some flour, what you would call an amount of perhaps one pound, four eggs and some cheese."

By this time the children were gathered round, all listening intently.

"Come on, Mum, let's let him try it," said Jimmy enthusiastically. The others nodded in agreement.

"Do you agree to his offer, Corporal?" she asked.

"Yeah, we'll give it a go."

---

3   ragazzi = children

"But, Major, what can you make with those ingredients?" queried Vera.

"Ah, I must whisper to you, for if my men hear what I say, they will become very excited."

He leant forward, put his hand to the side of his mouth, and whispered, "Tagliatelle."

"What?" asked Judith.

"Tagliatelle. It is the most loved food of northern Italians. It was invented almost five hundred years ago to look like the hair of a princess."

"Do it taste like hair?" asked Alfie.

The major laughed, "No, no it tastes like food from heaven. You will see."

"Come on, time to get back to work. There's lots left to do, and it will soon be dark," said Vera.

The next morning, before work started, Major Balzarini sidled up to Vera and said, "I will need a kitchen assistant for my cooking. Is one of your children capable of this?"

> **TRUE FACT?**
>
> It is said that *tagliatelle* was invented in 1487 at the command of a king who wanted a dish that mimicked the ribbon-like hairstyle of his bride.
>
> This is still celebrated in the city of Bologna, where there is a display of tagliatelle made of gold, showing the exact dimensions the strands should be – 1mm by 6mm.

"I would be interested myself to see you make your dish, but I need to drive the tractor. Judith, would you like to learn some Italian cooking?"

While the girl's efforts at potato planting on the previous day could not be faulted, she herself found the prospect of avoiding it today very attractive.

"Yes, Mum, that would be fun."

The corporal, seeing the chance to avoid another day in the cold and damp, reacted.

"I'll guard the major today, Jenkins. You stay here and guard the others."

Work started and the Italian, the corporal, and Judith retired to the house. The soldier sat on a chair in the kitchen while the major started to explain to Judith what she should do.

"First the tools we need. Can you find for me the wooden thing for this?"

He imitated rolling something on the table.

"Ah, a rolling pin. It's in the drawer. What else?"

"We must have a board to roll on, a sharp knife, and a fork."

When these were on the table, he continued. "Next, the ingredients. We will make enough for eight people. I see you have the device for weighing, we must have 500 grammes of flour, but the device only has pounds, so we can say, one pound."

Judith weighed out a pound of flour in the basin on the scale.

"Now, heap this flour onto the board. Unfortunately, this flour is not good for tagliatelle but it is all we have."

"What's wrong with it?" asked Judith.

"It should be much, much smaller pieces."

"Ah, finer you mean."

"Yes, we can make tagliatelle, but it will not be as soft as perfect pasta should be. And now, my dear Judith, we need four eggs."[4]

And so, the two continued with the process, while the guard, who had quickly lost interest, dozed in his chair.

The work was interrupted mid-morning by the need to make tea for the workers. Excitement was building among the children and Vera about the lunch to come, and it was hugely heightened when Judith came up from the house and surprised the Italian prisoners with an announcement.

"Listen, everyone, Judith has something to say!" shouted Vera.

Judith took a deep breath and then, as loudly as she could, announced what the major had taught her, *"Oggi a pranzo abbiamo tagliatelle".*[5]

There was a loud cheer from the three men.

The lunch proved to be a great success. The three prisoners ate outside, sitting on the garden bench, while the major dined with Vera and the children in the kitchen. Meanwhile, the two soldiers stood in the garden, enjoying their double ration of sandwiches.

"Well, how did you like the speciality of my region?" asked the major. "The cheese sauce is of my own invention."

The children looked at each other to see who was going to respond. Jimmy, outspoken as usual, commented.

"It was very nice, a bit slippery like, but all right."

Alfie added, "It don't stay on the fork too easy, do it?"

---

4 The full recipe appears at the end of this book

5 *Oggi a pranzo abbiamo tagliatelle* = Today for lunch we are having tagliatelle

Vera intervened and said, "Well, thank you for introducing us to tagliatelle. It was a special experience for us all."

The major was quite undaunted by the lack of enthusiasm and said, "Then tomorrow, I will make it again. Perhaps with a different sauce."

"I'm sorry, Luigi, I am afraid we can't spare the eggs. Do you know, the ration here is one egg a week for adults?"

"But, Signora Vera, I am a detective, I notice things. I saw that you have many eggs in your larder."

Vera was saved from replying when she was interrupted by the corporal, who came into the kitchen and said, "Ma'am, there's a car at the end of the track, the driver has got out to open the gate."

"Oh, I'm not expecting any visitors. Unless, unless…"

Vera got to her feet and looked out the window. She immediately recognised Mr Stevens's car.

CHAPTER 5

Three Shocks in One Day

As the car bumped along the stony track, Vera and the inquisitive children filed out of the house to await the vehicle's arrival. When it came to a halt in front of them, the driver's door opened and Mr Stevens stepped out.

"Good afternoon, Mrs Orton. As promised, I have arranged for Master Field to see his sister. She is in the car."

Lowering his voice, he said, "I need to discuss an urgent matter with you before I leave."

He opened the passenger door and a little girl, gripping a grubby doll, slid off the back seat and onto the ground.

Alfie stood open mouthed, gaping at his sister. "Pauline. It's Pauline."

The boy was too embarrassed to offer a hug to his sister, but she had no such inhibitions and threw her arms round him while still grasping the doll in one hand.

Vera had not moved, but she noticed what the girl's brother had not. The young child's dress had a tear on one side and was food stained, and she looked very thin and poorly nourished. Her hair, which had Vera seen it all those months ago, was once well groomed and crowned with a red ribbon, was unkempt and seemingly not recently washed. The woman glanced at Judith; there was no doubt that the girl had also noticed Pauline's appearance.

Vera broke her silence, "So, you are Pauline. Alfie has told us all about you. He was so worried when he lost you after you left the ferry."

"Me too, missus. I had to go to live with Mrs Parry."

Vera thought for a moment about what Pauline should call her and then said, "I'm Mrs Orton. This is Jimmy, my son, and over there is Judith. Just like you, she has had to leave her home and live with a new mum."

"I ain't got no new mum. I live with Mrs Parry and Mr Parry."

"Alfie, why don't you show Pauline around the farm? You can introduce her to your pony. In fact, I'll tell you what. You don't need to work this afternoon. Just have a nice time with Pauline and later we'll all have tea together."

"Right, Mum, she can collect the eggs with me."

Vera nodded and then turned to Mr Stevens. "You wanted to tell me something, well I have something to tell you too! Let's go into the house. The rest of you, off to work."

Mr Stevens followed Vera into the kitchen.

"Do sit down, Mr Stevens."

He pulled a chair out from the table and sat down.

"Now, Mrs Orton…."

"No, let me speak first. Did you not notice the state of that little girl? She is filthy, poorly dressed and clearly undernourished."

"Well, I have to say that I um.. I um, well, did notice a faint smell about her."

"Who are these Parry people? How could you place a child with such uncaring foster parents?"

"Well, Mrs Orton, I have to say, you are being a bit unfair. I don't choose the families. They are selected by the local authority according to how much space they have available in their homes. That inevitably means that some hosts are, how should I say, um, well that they are unenthusiastic about entertaining a guest."

Vera could not contain her anger. "But this is disgraceful! Surely, the criterion is wrong. First and foremost, the host should be capable of treating a guest in the same way as they treat their own children!"

"I'm afraid that this is not the way it works. And besides, Mrs Parry has no children of her own. But please hear me out. I have important news for you."

Vera seethed in silence and let Mr Stevens have his say.

"On January 10th, there was heavy bombing in Portsmouth. Commercial Road and the district around it was severely damaged. I am very sorry to have to tell you that I have been informed that the Field children's mother was killed."

> **TRUE FACTS**
>
> On January 10th, 1941, 300 German aircraft attacked Portsmouth. They dropped 350 tons of high explosive bombs and 25,000 incendiary devices designed to cause fires. There were 171 deaths and 431 people were injured. Three thousand people lost their homes. The Guildhall was among the buildings destroyed by fire, as damaged water supplies made firefighting impossible.

41

Vera remained silent for a few seconds, then said, "Oh my lord, poor Alfie and Pauline."

She paused and then said, "Why has it taken six weeks to tell me about this?"

"Yes, I deeply regret that, but in the general destruction the information about which children had lived in the house was lost. In fact, at first it was thought that the children had been killed too. When the authorities discovered the good news that the children were on the Island, we were asked to trace them. Of course, the children have missed their mother's funeral."

"But what about their father?"

"Mr Field is an artificer, that is a naval engineer, serving on active duty aboard *HMS Hood*. The War Office has informed him of the tragedy, but of course we are not allowed to be told where the ship is. It is most unlikely that he will be ashore for a very long time."

There was a long silence while they both considered the tragic situation the children were in. Suddenly, Vera thumped the table with her fist and said loudly, "Mr Stevens, forgive me for being direct. I would like you to drive to Freshwater, yes I know it's long way, but I want no excuses. Please drive to Freshwater, collect Pauline's belongings and her ration card and bring them back here. She is coming to live with me."

"Mrs Orton, I can assure that I would not make any excuses, this is a fine gesture."

Mr Stevens got up from the table to leave.

"Oh, Mr Stevens, this will of course mean even more driving for me, so perhaps you might use your influence to increase my diesel ration by few more gallons."

Mr Stevens gave a wry smile and, as he saw himself out, said, "Quite so, Mrs Orton. It is the least I can do."

Vera sat at the table simmering down after the conversation and considering the consequences of her impetuous kindness. Then she put her head in her hands and said aloud, "What have I done!"

There was a silence, then she added, "Beds! Organise that first. Then Pauline needs a scrubbing."

Ten minutes later, the tractor arrived at the potato field. Vera saw that Jimmy was working near to the far end of one of the long furrows, and Judith was walking towards where the seed sacks were, bucket in hand. Vera drove the tractor to meet her.

"Hello, Judith, getting a refill?"

"Yes, Mum. I am getting quicker at this, but I will be glad when it's finished."

"Won't we all! Judith, I need to have a chat with you. Wait for me to get down."

The girl came over to the tractor.

"Not tagliatelle again?" asked Judith with a broad smile.

Vera laughed and said, "No, no we've tried it and that will do for a while. No, I need to talk to you about a serious matter."

"Oh, what's wrong?"

"I saw that you noticed how untidy and unwashed little Pauline was."

"Yes, it was awful. Doesn't anyone look after her?"

"It seems not. I want to talk to you about her. I need your help. I have to give the little girl and Alfie some very bad news and I feel that I cannot simply send her back to the place where she has been living. I fear that she is not being cared for in a loving way."

"You don't mean…."

"Yes, I am afraid so. You are going to get a little sister."

"Oh. I see," said Judith with a distinct lack of enthusiasm.

"The fact is, Alfie and Pauline have lost their mother. She was killed in a bombing raid on Portsmouth in January."

Judith's jaw dropped. "Oh dear, oh dear. That's awful. What about their father?"

"He is on a naval ship, we don't know where, but it's probably a long way away.

"Poor Alfie."

"I know you didn't like it when I decided to let him live with us, did you?"

"No, but, well, I've got used to him."

"And you like him now, don't you?"

"Well, yes, most of the time. At least when he is newly bathed."

The two of them laughed and then Vera said, "I'm sure you will soon like Pauline too."

"So, how do you want me to help you?"

"That's the spirit. Today, there are two things we have to do. First of all, with Pauline. We have to give the girl a good scrub and get that tangled hair washed. So, we need to get bath water ready. We also need to wash her clothes and I see that I will need to do some repairs. Mr Stevens has gone to get all her other clothes and things. So, it is a bath day and a wash day. You can stop working here for the afternoon."

"What's the other thing?"

"I'm now going to talk to Jimmy. I'm going to offer to let him move to Uncle Don's old bedroom. It's much bigger than the one he has now, and it is on the ground floor. If he agrees to move, then you can choose to take his bedroom, it's bigger than yours and Pauline can take the one you have now."

"But what about using candles to light the room? Pauline is too small to use them safely."

"That's true, so I must make sure that I blow the light out when I tuck her in."

"Shall I go to the house now?"

"Yes, wait there for me there. I am going to talk to Jimmy and then I'll join you."

"See you soon."

"Oh, Judith, not a word to the children about their mother."

"Of course not."

Vera decided to play her secret weapon to encourage Judith's enthusiasm.

"Oh, Judith, Pauline will need a pony. I have a friend near Ventnor who has a Shetland, which her children have got too big for. I'm sure she will let us have it."

Judith smiled and said, "Oh, exciting!"

Shortly after, Vera took Jimmy aside and informed him of the situation. Initially, he was even more negative than Judith about the little girl moving in, but when he learnt of the death of her mother, he was far more understanding.

"Yes please, I'd love to move to the other bedroom. Uncle Don's wire aerial is connected to that room. I can use it with my wireless."

"Then I suggest that you stop work for the day and go to the house to start packing up your things."

The farmhouse erupted into activity. Before she went upstairs to start packing her things for a move into Jimmy's room, Judith had lit the fire in the bath house and filled the boiler with water. Jimmy himself, who had by far the most things to move, had started going up and down stairs as he moved his toys, books and clothes to his new bedroom. Vera was frantically directing the operation while at the same time getting to know Pauline. She had broken the news to Alfie and Pauline that from now on, brother and sister would both be staying at Cliff Top Farm. They were delighted. However, Vera decided to wait until a less hectic time to tell them the bad news about their mother.

"Alfie, why don't you go back to the field and do a little more work while I get to know Pauline and make arrangements for her. Do you remember where you had got to?

"Yes, I was doing the row on the top of the field near Churchfield farm, but you said I could be free this afternoon."

"Just carry on there for a little while and soon I'll send Jimmy to tell you when tea is ready."

"But, missus, where am I going to live?" asked Pauline, who was completely confused by all the activity going on around her.

Vera put an arm around her and said, "Now, I am going to show you. Come on upstairs with me. Bring your dolly too, she is going to live here with you. Then later it's bath time for you and dolly."

"Why? Is it Saturday?"

Vera laughed and said, "No, it's Tuesday, but you missed our Saturday bath night, so you can have yours today."

The side of the field, where they were planting potatoes, ran parallel with the cliff top which was behind a tangle of bushes and trees. Between these and the field there was a stretch of fairly flat grassland. The grass was kept permanently short by the rabbits, which inhabited hundreds of burrows in the soft chalk ground.

As Alfie was dragging his bucket along the furrow by the edge of the field, he became aware of a noise. It grew louder and louder. He looked up towards the sound.

"It must be an aeroplane," he thought, "and very close. But where is it?"

Suddenly, from behind a low hill on the next farm's land, the plane appeared. It was flying very low and directly towards Alfie. It streaked past him, following the grassy area beside the cliff and then started to climb. The Italians, further away in the field, had stopped working and, together with the two soldiers, watched as the plane made a wide turn and flew off in the direction it had come from. Everyone started work again but there was much chattering between them about what they had just seen.

Just a few minutes later, Alfie heard the noise again and then the aircraft appeared once more from the same direction, this time flying much more slowly. The engine noise was now uneven and there were popping sounds as it approached. It was getting lower and lower. Then its wheels touched the grassy surface, the plane hopping and bouncing as it landed. It came to a halt, almost by the side of Alfie. He stood rivetted to the spot. The sign on the side of

---

TRUE FACTS

The Messerschmitt 109 was probably the best German fighter plane of the Second World War. Over 34,000 of them were built.

The only British plane that could match the 109 was the Spitfire. Both planes had advantages and disadvantages over each other.

---

the plane was a black cross with a white surround. On the tail was a swastika. He was aghast, it was a German plane!

Had he been facing the other direction he would have seen that the two soldiers, a considerable distance from him, were pointing their rifles at the plane and shouting to the Italians to move out of the way. The engine stopped and the cover on the high cockpit of the Messerschmitt 109 was pushed open.

CHAPTER 6

A German Guest

The transparent cockpit hood folded open and the head of a man wearing a brown leather flying helmet appeared out of the opening. He looked down and saw Alfie peering up at him.

"Good afternoon, young man. Have you come to accept my surrender?"

Alfie stared up, open mouthed. He thought of running away, but this was just too interesting. He ran his eyes over the fuselage of the plane and saw that there was a line of holes running across part of it.

He blurted out, "You been shot?"

"Only slightly, young sir, but your Spitfire made much damage to my beautiful plane."

Alfie watched as, with difficulty, the pilot climbed on to the wing of the plane. He was clearly only able to use one arm. With his good hand he struggled to stuff something into his jacket pocket. It was when he jumped to the ground that Alfie saw that the left sleeve of his leather jacket had a gaping hole and there was blood around it.

"Vot is your name, young man?" asked the tall figure in front of him.

"Alfred Field, sir."

"Ah, Alfred, a good German name. Young Alfred Field, I must surrender my pistol to you before those two soldiers over there decide to shoot both of us."

Alfie looked behind him and saw that the soldiers were kneeling, some distance away, with their rifles pointed at the plane.

"However, first it is my duty to try to destroy my plane."

Alfie watched as the pilot struggled to pull something out of the pocket of his jacket.

"Alfred, be so kind as to help me. Hold the coat straight while my signal pistol I pull out."

Alfie did as he was asked, and the man managed to take out a gun with a very wide barrel. Alfie noticed that the man had also pulled out some pieces of paper from the pocket. The wind took them, but the pilot paid no attention.

"This is the gun I use if I land in the sea and need help. It shoots red stars. We must move away from the plane, young Alfred. Or we may be burned."

He took a few steps, pushing Alfie in front of him, and then turned and aimed the pistol in the direction of the plane. There was a whoosh as a red flash shot across and landed on the side of the aircraft. It bounced off, barely scorching the paint and the burning red mass fell sizzling to the ground and burnt out.

"There happens nothing, the petroleum tank is empty."

"Why must you burn it?" asked Alfie.

"The Luftwaffe does not want the British about our planes to learn. But I was unsuccessful. Now you must take my real pistol. The famous Mauser gun."

He unclipped a holster on his hip and took out the weapon. Alfie watched, wide eyed as the pilot slid his thumb up to a switch at the back of the pistol. As he did so, a metal tube slid out of the handle and fell to the ground, scattering bullets.

"Now it is safe. This you can hold and march me to the soldiers over there."

He held his right hand in the air and started walking through the mud, though much hampered by his heavy flying boots. Alfie walked behind, holding the pistol in one hand and his bucket in the other.

News of the event had spread quickly. A small crowd of watchers had appeared from Churchfield farm, everyone cautiously keeping a distance from the plane. The sound of a tractor indicated that Vera had also been alerted.

"Put both hands up!" shouted Corporal Trent as he stood, pointing his rifle at the pilot.

"He can't, he got shot in the arm!" shouted Alfie.

It was quickly obvious to the soldiers that the prisoner presented no threat to them.

"Better put that pistol away, Alfie," called the soldier.

Alfie threw the gun into his bucket.

The pilot saluted the corporal and very crisply said, "Oberleutnant[6] Hans Seitz, surrendering as a prisoner of war."

The private turned to the corporal and said, "What do we do now?"

---

6   Oberleutnant = First lieutenant

51

"Well, we have to get reinforcements. We can't guard four Italians and a German. We ought to guard the plane too, before souvenir hunters start stealing bits of it."

As they were talking, Vera arrived.

"You all right, Alfie?"

"Yeah, Mum, it was amazing. Super, super amazing! I got to carry the gun!"

The pilot turned to Vera and said, "You have a most fine son, Frau[7] Field."

"Shut up, you, and keep your hand up," snapped the corporal.

"Corporal, can't you see, the man is wounded? What do you propose to do now?"

"It is my intention, Mrs Orton, to march the Italians back to the guest house to get reinforcements. Meanwhile, the private will guard the plane."

"And what about your prisoner?"

"Um, I must seek medical support."

"And meanwhile?"

"Er…well, he will have to wait here."

Vera laughed. "Bring him to the house, I have some first aid things. Come on, Alfie, jump up beside me, bring your bucket." She climbed back onto the tractor, turned it round, and drove off.

Later, the children watched as the pilot was brought into the kitchen by the soldiers. The posters they saw every day in the town and the dreadful stories they heard about the Nazis had led them to expect some ghoulish figure to emerge through the doorway, but the man who came in was quite a

---

7   Frau = Mrs

normal looking figure. There was nothing unusual about him at all now that he had taken off his flying helmet and given it to Alfie to wear. However, he did have a cut on his forehead.

"We will have to leave him with you, Mrs Orton. It's a pity you have no telephone."

"That's all right, Corporal. I don't think a one-armed man is a threat to us."

"Alfie, what did you do with that pistol?" asked the soldier.

"It's in the bucket outside."

"I'll get it for you, Mrs Orton."

"Good heavens, I don't need a gun to guard him."

Unaware that the pilot had emptied the bullets from the pistol, he said, "I'll bring it in anyway, in case there is trouble."

After the soldier had left, Vera, forcing herself to sound friendly, said, "Come and sit down. I'll put some plaster on your head. How did you get that bump?"

The pilot laughed and said, "My landing was incorrect, the ground was not like a runway."

Vera was going through a terrible mental torment. Here was a member of the very same air force which had killed Alfie and Pauline's mother. She had not yet even broken the news to the children. But she found that in all conscience she could not refuse to help this injured enemy. She dabbed the cut with antiseptic and then put on some cotton wool under a piece of sticking plaster.

"Now let's look at your left arm. Jimmy, help him off with his jacket."

"You are very kind, Frau Field, but that is not necessary. My wound is not deep, I was lucky, the shot just touched me. I can a plaster put on."

The man started to stand up.

53

"Don't be silly, I'll do it."

"No, I repeat, it is not necessary. This is not something the children should see. If you give me some plaster and the bathroom show me, I will do it, I can use my right hand."

Vera gave an exasperated sigh and then said, "Jimmy, show our visitor where the lavatory is."

A few minutes later, the pilot returned.

"Do sit down. We are waiting for some soldiers to come to take you away. What did you say your name was?" asked Vera.

"My name is Hans Seitz."

"You speak good English," said Judith.

"Thank you, Fräulein[8]. I should, for I am a teacher of school children."

"Why are you flying a fighter plane then?" asked Jimmy.

"Before this war, flying was my hobby. When the war began, of my free will I joined the Luftwaffe - the German Air Force. But I was careful not to be a bomber pilot."

"Why?" asked Vera.

"Why? Mrs Field, have you not heard of the terrible punishment innocent people receive from English bombs in Germany and I think too from German bombs in Britain?"

Vera, paused, trying to control her feelings, before she quietly answered, "Yes, Hans, we have. Alfie and Judith and little Pauline are living with me precisely because of these awful bombings of the cities where they normally live. My name is Mrs Orton by the way, not Mrs Field."

"But you kill people with your plane!" exclaimed Jimmy.

---

8   Fräulein = Miss, form of address for a single woman

"Yes, it can happen. But then the fight is between military people, not civilians. It is pilot against pilot."

"What happened to your plane, what are them holes in the side?" asked Alfie.

"Today, it was not a good day for me. I test a new system to find our way, to navigate to cities in England and I did not see a lone Spitfire. The pilot was most clever, he flew with behind him, the bright sun and I was too slow to notice."

"So, what happened?"

"He hit my plane, but not too badly. He made a hole in my fuel tank, this was a big problem for me. As you saw, Alfred, I only just had enough petroleum to land in your field."

"Well, your appearance here has certainly caused some excitement," said Vera.

"The private said that there were people gathered around the plane just waiting to grab souvenirs," commented Jimmy.

Then, suddenly, Hans sat up straight and banged his right hand on the table.

"Donner und blitzen! What a fool I am!"

"That means "thunder and lightning,", said Judith.

"Yes, Fräulein. You are right."

"What have you done?" she asked.

"In my hurry to surrender to Alfred, I have most important documents in the plane forgotten and the thing most terrible is that with the documents are the photos of my wife and children."

"You have children?"

"Yes, a boy about your age and little girl. They both have hair the same colour as yours," he replied pleasantly. Then he became very agitated and said sternly, "I must have these documents, they are very important."

"There is nothing we can do about it now," said Vera.

"But I must destroy the documents and also if I am to live in an English prison for years, I must have the photos. They are dear to me."

"I don't think there is a chance that the private will let us get on to the plane," said Jimmy.

"Please, please try."

"Jimmy, go and see if he will let you have a look. Take him a slice of the cake I made yesterday; it might make him more friendly."

"Where in the cockpit are the documents?" asked Jimmy.

"Oh, you are so kind. They are under the seat of the pilot in a black cover."

The boy wrapped the cake in a piece of paper and stood up to leave.

"Put the kettle on, Judith, I'm sure Mr Seitz is thirsty. Jimmy, wait outside a moment, I need to talk to you."

Vera left the kitchen and, outside the front door, she said in a low voice to the boy, "If you are able to get the documents, just give him the photos when you get back. We must stop him destroying anything the army might want to see."

"How exciting," he said as he hurried off to the field.

CHAPTER 7

Recovering the Documents

"Hello, Jimmy, come to have a look at the plane?" said Private Jenkins.

"Well, yes, but not really just to look. Um, you see the pilot has left some stuff in the cockpit that he needs to take with him when he gets locked up."

"Why should we help him? He's an enemy and a dangerous one at that, the first one we've caught, by the way. I might get promotion for this, he's an officer."

"But he needs some papers to show your officers when they interrogate him."

"Um…well I can't go up into the plane. Look at that lot over there," he said, pointing at the crowd that had assembled on the grass a short distance from the aircraft. As soon as I move they are going to start breaking bits off the plane as valuable souvenirs."

"You can't stay here all night," said Jimmy.

"No, when they send reinforcements there will be a couple of blokes to stand guard. I expect that the technicians will come too to take out the radio and other equipment to see if they can learn any new information."

"Oh, I forgot. Mum sent you a bit of cake. She thought you might be getting hungry."

"That's very kind of her, say thanks from me."

"So, can you help me?"

"Well to get into the cockpit you'll have to climb up on the wing and you'll have to grow a bit to do that!"

"Can you bunk me up?"

"Come on then. Wait while I put my rifle and cake down."

The wing slanted down at the back edge and Jimmy was quickly up on to it. He then clambered up to open the cockpit and climbed over the side. He found himself in a tight compartment where there was hardly space for even a boy to stand, so he sat in the pilot's seat and looked around him. He was surprised that the cockpit was completely undamaged. There were two foot pedals and masses of dials on a dashboard. In front of him was a lever with some controls on it.

"You all right Jimmy?" called the private.

"Yes, just looking around."

"Hurry up, it will be dark soon."

Jimmy suddenly recalled why he was there. He put his hand under the seat but felt nothing. Then, looking at the floor, he realised that there was a black cover under one of the pedals. It must have slid forward when the plane landed. He picked it up and climbed back over the side and on to the wing.

"What a minute, Jimmy, I'll help you," said the private.

"It's ok, I can jump down."

"Did you find it?" asked the soldier.

"I think so, I'll go and show it to him."

"You'd better hurry, I saw a staff car and a truck arrive just now. They are probably taking him away. Oh, by the way, I found this in the grass. You'd better take that too."

He handed Jimmy a crumpled, folded piece of paper that had got muddied, probably by the private's boots. He stuffed it in his pocket.

"Thanks. See you tomorrow," said Jimmy as he hurried off to the house. On his way, he passed two soldiers, carrying rifles, on their way to the plane.

As he got nearer, he saw an officer's car and a lorry driving off down the track away from the house. He was too late to give the pilot his photos.

"Has he gone, Mum?"

"Yes and thank goodness for that. We haven't finished moving the beds and all the stuff from your room and the others too. Pauline is tired and needs an early night, and I am expecting Mr Stevens at any minute with her stuff. I haven't even started the supper yet."

"I haven't fed the sows, either."

"Are those the papers he wanted?"

"I suppose so, they were the only ones I could find."

"Put them in the cupboard, we'll give them to the corporal tomorrow."

"Mum, would you like me to make the supper?" asked Judith.

"That's very kind of you to offer. I hadn't decided yet what we should have. Not that there is much choice."

"I thought I could bake some potatoes in the oven, like I've seen you do. Can you spare some cheese? I could grate it and then slice the potatoes when I take them out of the oven and put the cheese in."

Vera threw her arms around the girl and exclaimed, "Judith Neville, four months ago you did not know how to boil an egg, and now look at you! Yes, darling, a lovely idea for supper. Don't burn your fingers. Jimmy, just this evening could you do the mash for horses so that Judith can do the cooking?"

"I suppose so. I hear a car!"

"Ah, that must be Mr Stevens."

Vera went to the front door.

"Come in, Mr Stevens, forgive the disorganised state we are in, it has been a rather busy day."

He followed Vera into the kitchen and said, "Here is such property as the young lady has."

He put a homemade rucksack onto the table and, as he did so, he noticed something else on it.

"Is that a gun, Mrs Orton?"

"Oh yes, I'd forgotten about it."

"But, but why do you have it? It looks like a German luger pistol."

Vera picked up the gun and put into the cupboard on top of the black document cover.

"It's a very long story, do sit down and I'll explain."

As she talked, she occasionally cast glances at Judith as the girl busied about preparing supper, and she felt some satisfaction and even pride that the city girl had progressed so far.

At length, Mr Stevens said, "I can see that this has been a tumultuous day for you, I mustn't detain you further."

As Vera walked to the front door with him, he said, "I note that you have a car parked outside. I take it that you will be needing a petrol allowance as well as diesel for the tractor."

"That would be very helpful, Mr Stevens."

"I'll see what I can do."

As soon as the front door was closed, she returned to the kitchen and opened the rucksack on the table.

"I can see that we have more laundry to do tomorrow, Judith."

The girl laughed as she said, "I think I would prefer to plant potatoes."

"Now, Alfie and Pauline, I would like to talk with you. Let's go up to Alfie's room," suggested Vera.

Thoughts

Alfie drifted off to sleep much more slowly than usual. There had just been such excitement today.

"It was a real, really real plane that landed beside me. Perhaps I should have been scared. Come to think of it I was, but the want to see it was so big I never was frightened. I had seen so many planes in the air, but they were far away. This was up close! And it was German! The pilot weren't so unfriendly like what I expected, what was good because he had a gun. I was surprised how heavy it was. Wait till I tell my real mum, and dad too. It's good to be with Pauline again but she can be a nuisance because I have to explain things and take care of her. She's too little to have jobs on the farm, she'll have to help me, but she better not break any eggs."

When Judith blew out the oil lamp she crept into her new bed and snuggled under the covers.

"What would my real mother have said if she had seen me cook supper for a whole family? They seemed to like it, but Pauline only ate half. Never mind, Alfie and Jimmy shared out what she left. How is Mum going to tell Alfie and Pauline about their real mother? The German pilot seemed a nice man, but he can't be really or he would not be fighting against England. The Italians are enemies too, but they are so funny and happy I can't imagine them fighting us. Giuseppe sings beautifully. Carlo looks like the bandit in a comic but even he laughs a lot and works hard. Gosh we all work hard. Mum says we will be finished with this job by tomorrow, Thursday. I hope that I can get the Shetland pony for Pauline on Friday. But how? It will be too small for me to ride. I had hoped to practise my German with the pilot, but he was taken away by the soldiers before he finished his tea. Why wouldn't he let Mum put a plaster on his arm? I hope we can go riding on Saturday. This room is very nice, but now that Jimmy has taken all his books and things the shelves are all bare. I must ask Mum if she has any ornaments I can put on them."

Jimmy lay in bed and reached out to turn off the bedside lamp.

"It's strange having an electric lamp. I wonder how Judith is getting on with the spirit lamp? An unbelievable day today. Wait till I tell my friends at school that I sat in the cockpit of a fighter plane, and a German one at that. It's strange that there were no bullet holes where the pilot sat because he said one grazed his arm. There was definitely a hole in his flying jacket sleeve. It was a pity that he didn't get the photos of his family. It would be interesting to see what

they look like. I must look in that black folder tomorrow before we give it to the soldiers. Oh! I forgot to look at that piece of paper that the private gave to me. The pilot must have dropped it. We should finish the potatoes in one more day. Next week, when we start school again, Mum will drive us in the Austin Seven. I can't wait to see my friends' faces when we arrive!"

Vera sat in the wooden armchair by the side of coal oven, a cup of Horlicks in hand. She had opened the iron door on the side of the oven to enjoy the burning coal's full heat. As she watched the glowing red lumps, she thought back over the day's events.

"The war seems to be becoming very real now. Columns of army lorries, some towing big guns, even some tanks have been passing along the road by the farm track towards Ventnor. I don't want to frighten the children, but it looks like a big operation. Poor Mr Stevens! I shouldn't have taken out my anger on him. It's true what he said, he didn't make the rules for choosing suitable families to take in evacuees. Anyway, I don't think he will allow any more children to be placed with Mr and Mrs Parry. Oh dear, oh dear, poor Alfie and Pauline. How am I going to tell them about their mother? I think I'll wait until Friday and tell them just before we go to get the Shetland. Hopefully, getting the new pony will cheer them up. I'll drive the children there and the four of them can lead the animal back to the farm. I'll take the tack back in the car. Perhaps the walk will be too far for Pauline. The Italians have been a great help, not that Luigi does much. When we have finished the potatoes, I am going to ask if they can check and repair the fencing round the pastures. Unbelievable! A German pilot in my kitchen! He was friendly enough, but there was something a bit strange, he

was almost too friendly. The soldiers who collected him were a bit rough. It must have hurt his arm. But then that was a bit odd too, I never saw the wound. Why didn't he want me to? Let's hope that tomorrow is a little less eventful and that we can finish planting the potatoes. Goodness knows how I am going to find time to finish rearranging the rooms and give Pauline a little love."

CHAPTER 8

The Black Folder Is Opened

"Is Pauline still asleep, Alfie?"

"Dunno, Mum. I come straight to breakfast."

"Jimmy, get the rest of the things ready while I go to wake the little one and get her dressed. Bread and dripping this morning."

"Hurrah, my favourite. I'll stoke up the boiler so that we can make some toast to put the meat fat on."

"Put some salt on the table for those who want it. Oh, good morning, Judith, can you help Jimmy while I get Pauline?"

"Good morning, Mum. Have you put the kettle on Jimmy?"

It was while the two of them were engaged in breakfast preparations that they became aware of the sound of a lorry coming up the farm track. Jimmy opened the kitchen curtain.

"It's an army lorry, no, two of them and there is an officer's car too."

They both watched as the lorries passed the house and continued up the grassy track in the direction of the potato field. The staff car stopped outside the house. The door opened and the passenger, a figure in a smart uniform with a leather strap across his chest, put on his cap and opened the front gate.

Jimmy went into the hall and called up the stairs, "Mum, we have a visitor."

At the same time there was a loud knock at the door.

"Answer the door, Jimmy!" shouted a voice from upstairs.

"Good morning, young man. May I speak with your mother?"

"She's just coming, sir. Do come in."

"No, I can wait here."

A few seconds later Vera came down the stairs hand in hand with Pauline.

"Good morning, Captain Morley. How can I help you?"

"Good morning. Mrs Orton. I am just calling as a matter of courtesy to inform you that army technicians will be working on the aircraft on your land."

"Are they going to remove it?"

"No, they will be inspecting the equipment on the plane and taking parts away for analysis. It shouldn't take more than a day."

"What happens then?"

"Sometime next week our engineers will come to cut up the plane and remove the scrap."

"Will your men be guarding it until then?"

"No, it won't be necessary once we have removed the equipment today."

"Well, thank you for letting me know."

"That is the least I could do in view of the inconvenience to you of having an enemy aircraft on your land. Goodbye, Mrs Orton."

"Goodbye, Captain. Oh, Captain, I wanted to ask if the Italians can continue to do other tasks around the farm next week?"

"Yes, of course. They can work here as long as you need them."

"Thank you, goodbye."

Vera took Pauline with her into the kitchen.

"You sit over there, dear," she said to Pauline. "Alfie, get some breakfast for your sister. Now, I realise that I don't need to tell Judith and Jimmy what the captain had to say because I'm certain you were both listening to every word."

Amid the laughter, Vera added, "It has rained overnight so the field will be muddy, but we should get this job done if only I can find the time to do the ploughing."

"Mum, I've got an idea."

"Oh, tell us."

"Well, since you have lots to do with the rearranging of the rooms and looking after Pauline, why don't you ask Carlo to drive the tractor? He's a farmer, he must be able to drive a tractor."

"He has been watching what you have been doing, so he must know what to do," said Judith.

"Not a bad idea, Jimmy. I'll discuss it with Luigi. Now hurry up to get your chores here done and then go up to the field."

"Oh, by the way, it was the seventh day," said Judith.

"What do you mean?" asked Jimmy.

"You know, Mum asked, 'On which day had they planted half the field?'"

"Oh goodness me, I had forgotten that. When did I ask you?"

"It was on Monday morning, Mum."

"Well, Judith, you are right. Can you explain to the others how you worked that out?"

"The farmer planted double so many each day, so if he finished the field on the eighth day, he must have doubled the number of the day before – day seven."

"Oh, clever clogs, Judith," groaned Jimmy.

Laughing, they all departed to get on with their chores.

The day turned out to be much less eventful than Wednesday had been. Although Vera had at first been nervous about Carlo driving her beloved tractor, she soon realised that he was indeed used to such work. That gave her some time to get to know Pauline and finish the arrangements in the house. Jimmy and Alfie were much distracted by the work going on by the plane and, eventually, they could not resist going to watch the army technicians as they dismantled bits of machinery and the instruments in the cockpit.

A panel, the whole side of the front of the plane, had been opened up. "Is that the engine?" asked Jimmy, pointing at a jumble of pipes and a construction that reminded him of part of the tractor.

"Yes, sonny, a beauty it is too. German engineering is first class."

"Is there anything wrong with it?"

"No, it's in good order, it could be flown away now," said the engineer.

"But the petrol tank has got bullet holes in it, hasn't it?"

"Not that I can see," he answered.

"Jimmy, Alfie come on. Let's get this finished!" shouted a girl's voice.

By late afternoon, the last potatoes were in the ground. The Italians celebrated by singing in chorus with Giuseppe, while the children, who had been promised a special teatime, cleared up the empty sacks as the army lorries trundled down the uneven slope back to the farm track. The once proud plane stood abandoned and emptied of the vital parts the technicians wanted to inspect more closely in their workshop.

"Off you go and get washed. Jimmy, help Alfie, his nails are filthy. When you get back, there will be hot milk and a piece of home baked sponge cake," called Vera as the children trouped in.

When they returned, the older children joined Pauline at the kitchen table.

"Well, that's it. The potatoes are planted, now we don't need to do anything until we earth them up in April and I can do that with the tractor."

"What's 'earthing up,' Mum?" asked Judith.

"When the shoots appear, we push soil up on top of the potato plant by making a ridge of earth."

"But you'll need our help for the potato picking," said Jimmy.

"That's a long way off and at least the weather will be nicer then. Come on, let's cut the cake."

After tea, they all sat chattering a while before they started their farm chores.

"Mum, why do you think the pilot wouldn't let you put a plaster on his arm?"

"Well, he said that it was not a nice thing for you children to see."

Judith started laughing and then said, "It couldn't be worse than watching you skinning a rabbit!"

"Do you really think that he had bullet wound on his arm?"

"Why do you ask, Jimmy?"

"Well, I sat in the pilot's seat and looked around, there was no sign of any holes in the sides or the window."

"Are you sure? He must have been shot at while he was flying the plane," said Judith.

"Heavens above! I forgot all about his papers. I should have given them to the captain earlier today. Oh goodness me! I still have the pistol too! I must tell the corporal tomorrow."

"Let's have a look at the documents before we give them to him!" said Jimmy.

"I'm not sure that we should, they might be private," answered Vera.

"But he was quite happy for me to go to get them!" protested Jimmy.

"Please, Mum, it would be interesting to see his family photos," said Judith.

"Oh, all right then. Just a peek at them," said Vera, who was as inquisitive as the children.

Jimmy got off his chair and went over to get the black file. He came back and put it on the table.

"Careful, Jimmy, let me open it," said Vera. She carefully untied a string, wound round a small metal catch on the file, and then opened it. By this time all the children, except Pauline, were grouped at Vera's shoulder, peering over.

"See, there are two envelopes, one very thick one and one very thin. Which shall we open?"

"Stop, Mum, let me read what it says on the big envelope," pleaded Judith.

"Can you translate the German, Judith?" asked Jimmy.

"Can you? You done it before," said Alfie.

"Let me look at it, please."

Printed across the top of the envelope in big letters, it said –

Streng geheim

"What's that mean Judith?"

"Mum, that's a bit scary."

"Well, what does it mean?" demanded Jimmy.

"It says, 'Private Secret.'"

"What, like 'Top Secret'?"

"Yes, that's right, 'Top Secret.'"

"And what about them smaller words underneath?" said an excited Alfie.

Unternehmen Seelöwe

"I don't know what that means, they are new words for me."

"Have you got a dictionary?" asked Jimmy.

"No, you know very well that I only had a small rucksack when I arrived. There was no room for books."

"Gosh, look at the time!" exclaimed Vera. "Come on, you have chores to do. I'll keep the file for another day, and we can have another look tomorrow."

"Oh, Mum, please," pleaded Jimmy.

"No, you have the pigs to feed, and I want you to go down to the pasture to check the cows, before it gets dark. Alfie, off to the geese and hens with you."

"Can Jimmy help me to get some more hay from the loft in the stable, Mum?"

"Yes, of course. Oh, by the way, in all the excitement I almost forgot, you'll have an extra pony to feed tomorrow evening. We have the Shetland pony to collect. It's a mare called Daisy."

"Whoopee!" exclaimed Judith.

"But how are we going to get her here?" asked Jimmy.

"First thing tomorrow morning I have to show the Italians what work I want them to do. Then we will all squeeze into the car and drive to my friend's farm. I'll drop you three off and put all the pony's tack in the car with Pauline to drive home."

"How can we get home?" asked Alfie.

"You'll walk with the pony."

"Walk! What all the way?"

Jimmy laughed and said, "Don't worry, Alfie, it's not very far, about half an hour's walk."

"Now be off with you! Jobs to do!"

CHAPTER 9

An Army Visitor

On Friday morning, the corporal and Luigi appeared at the farmhouse just after breakfast.

"Good morning, Ma'am. What work do you want the men to do next?" asked the soldier.

"Good morning, Corporal, good morning, Major. I'd like the men to check and repair all the fencing round the two pastures. I'll drive down to meet you by the farm track gate. I'll bring a sledgehammer, staples, and tools and show the men what has to be done," said Vera.

By the time she returned to the house, the children had finished their tasks.

"How many eggs did you find, Pauline?" she asked.

The little girl counted the eggs in Alfie's basket.

"'ere, Pauline, be careful, don't touch them," demanded Alfie.

"Well? How many?"

"More than lots, perhaps ten," said the little girl.

Vera laughed and said, "Listen, everyone, I had an idea. Why don't we drive down to Ventnor, before we get Daisy, and visit the library?"

"What for?" asked Jimmy.

"To take out a German - English dictionary. That is, if they have one."

"Yes, yes then I can look up the words on the envelope!" said Judith.

"Exactly! Come on, let's get ready to go. I must get these muddy boots off and have a wash."

Soon after, Judith, Alfie, and Pauline squeezed into the back seat of the Austin. It was meant to be for two people, but the little girl managed to wedge herself between the others. Jimmy sat beside his mother.

The car bounced its way down the bumpy farm track to the main road. They turned left and headed for town. As they descended the steep hill, they could see the town in front of them, and they were soon outside the library.

"Judith, you come with me. Jimmy, you'll have to get out to make way for her. You stay with the other children."

"Can't we come, Mum?" asked Alfie.

"No, in the library you have to be absolutely quiet, and I think that would be impossible for you three. We won't be long."

A short while later, the two of them returned, Judith carrying a thick book.

"We've got it!"

"It's very fat," said Alfie.

"Well, there are a lot of words in a language," answered Judith as she climbed into the back of the car.

Vera drove the car out of the town and started up the long hill. As it climbed the slope the car went slower and slower until it was hardly moving at all and just made small jerky movements.

"What's wrong?" asked Judith.

"I'm afraid that Tim is protesting about having so many passengers. Give him some encouragement!"

"Come on, Tim!" they shouted.

"Come on, push!"

It was clear that the old car had seen better days.

Vera moved as best she could into the side of the road, pulled on the handbrake, and stopped the engine.

"Jimmy, you and Alfie walk up the hill, I'll wait for you at the top."

The boys got out and Vera started the car. It reluctantly pulled away and slowly gained speed.

Eventually, the boys caught up with the waiting car and jumped in. When they arrived at Vera's friend's farm, they immediately saw the Shetland pony, tied to the fence in front of the farmhouse.

"Oh, she's a grey," said Judith.

"No she ain't, she's white."

"Yes, Alfie, but white horses are called grey, aren't they, Mum?"

"That's true. Wait here while I talk to my friend."

Twenty minutes later, Vera drove off and the older children started their walk, with Jimmy holding the leading rein. Before they arrived at Cliff Top Farm, a boy of about sixteen passed them on a red bicycle. He had a dark-blue uniform and a round hat of the same colour. Soon after, he passed them again, cycling in the opposite direction. As he did so, he shouted, "You got a telegram!"

"Come on, Daisy, hurry up a bit. Let's see what the telegram is about," called Jimmy.

As they walked through the open farm gate, the Italian prisoners working on the fencing called greetings to them.

"Piccolo cavallo incantevole!" shouted Carlo.

"What did he say, Luigi?" asked Judith.

"He said, 'Lovely little horse.'"

Judith smiled with pride. Even though it wasn't to be her pony, she already felt responsible for Daisy.

"Come on, Judith, let's take Daisy to meet the other horses. We can let them all out into the paddock this afternoon," said Jimmy.

TRUE FACTS

In the 1940s very few people had a telephone so the only way to send an urgent message was by telegram. These were messages telegraphed by sending text over a phone line from post office to post office. The receiving office would print out the message and this would usually be delivered by a "telegram boy". Most of these boys were aged 14 to 18. They worked six days a week and a half day on Sundays. A typical wage was 15 shillings and eight pence a week (equivalent to 78 pence).

The telegram boys wore a navy-blue uniform with red piping round the jacket cuffs and the collar. Their round hats were of the same colour, with red edging. Each morning the boys were inspected by the postmaster, who checked that their black ties were straight and their shoes polished.

Telegrams had to be handed personally to the recipient, and the boy would have to wait to see if this recipient wanted to send a reply. The cost to send a telegram was six pence for nine words, (two and a half new pence).

As they approached the house, Vera and Pauline came out to meet them. The woman had a paper in her hand.

"Judith! I have a surprise for you!"

The girl left Jimmy to take the pony into the stable for a feed and went over to see Vera, who was waving a telegram in the air.

"It's from your mother. Guess what? She is coming to visit you tomorrow!"

"What, here?"

"Yes, she is coming on the three-thirty train. She has asked me to meet her at the station."

"But we were going riding tomorrow afternoon."

Vera laughed. "Surely, you can make time to see your mother!"

Judith was embarrassed when she said, "Of course, sorry, I didn't think about what I was saying."

"We can have a ride on Sunday instead. Does your mother ride?"

"No, she always watches me."

"Then she can do so here too. I think that you will have to share Pauline's room for a couple of nights and your mother can sleep in your room."

"How long is she staying?"

"For two days, though she says in the telegram that she has to do some work."

There was great excitement in the house on Saturday morning, though there were several moans as Vera insisted that the weekly clean should be more thorough than usual, on account of a visitor coming. At three o'clock Vera set off for town in light rain, with Judith and Pauline, leaving Jimmy and Alfie on the farm. After they had been to the fishmongers, they drove to the station.

"Here comes the train!" called Judith with excitement as the engine appeared through the tunnel in a great cloud of smoke.

With much squeaking of brakes, the train stopped by the platform.

"Ventnor, Ventnor. End of the line!" bawled a man in a blue uniform standing in front of them.

Some carriage doors opened, and people started to alight. Judith ran up and down the platform until she spotted a woman in a khaki jacket and skirt with a cap of the same colour.

"Mummy!" she called and ran to embrace her mother.

"Gosh, you have grown, darling. Your school uniform is almost too small for you!"

"But why are you wearing a uniform?"

"I'll explain later, dear. You must be Mrs Orton," she said, turning to Vera, who was standing holding Pauline's hand.

"So pleased to meet you, Mrs Neville, do please call me Vera."

"I'm Veronica. And this is your little daughter?"

"No, this is Pauline, another evacuee."

"Golly, you do have your hands full."

"There's another one too, Mummy. Pauline's brother, Alfie."

"Come on, let's get out of the rain. My car is outside. Judith, can you carry your mother's bag, she has her hands full with the umbrella and the briefcase."

"But, Mummy, why are you wearing a uniform?"

"Well, you know that I was working for the army when we were in London. That reminds me, I must talk to you about the house and getting new things for you. It is frightfully difficult to buy things now with rationing."

"You were saying about your uniform."

"Yes, darling, I can't tell you very much, it is all hush hush. But because of the sort of work I was doing, I was drafted into the army. I'm a lieutenant."

"Gosh, almost as important as Daddy."

They continued chatting while Vera drove through the town.

Soon the Austin was making its way up the hill, but all was not well.

"I'm sorry, Veronica, poor Tim finds this slope a bit much with passengers."

"Tim?"

"We call the car Tim, because it's tiny."

Vera stopped by the side of the road.

"Oh dear, what do we do now?" asked Veronica.

"Judith, can you take Pauline and walk up to the top. I'll wait for you there."

Veronica got out and folded the front seat down so that the other two could climb out, and then she put it back and sat down.

"Judith, darling, do take my umbrella or you will get soaked. You know how easily you catch cold."

Vera coaxed the car slowly up the hill.

"Judith is very prone to coughs and sneezes, she is quite a delicate child," said her mother.

Vera smiled as she thought of the sight of Judith planting potatoes in the muddy field, never complaining about the weather.

After picking up the two girls, they were soon driving through the open farm gates. Vera slowed to take a quick look at the cows clustered around the watering trough on the other side of the fence. They were mooing at being disturbed by the small car.

"Are they yours?"

"Yes, they like peace and quiet, not cars driving past."

"I've fed them, Mummy."

"What, you went into that mucky field?"

"Well, I did have boots on!"

Veronica stayed silent as the car drove up to the house.

"Welcome to Cliff Top Farm, Veronica!" said Vera.

Jimmy and Alfie came out to welcome the new arrival.

"This is my son, Jimmy and my evacuee son, Alfie."

"Pleased to meet you," said Jimmy.

"Hello, Missus, you Judith's mum?" asked Alfie.

"I am, indeed, young man."

"Jimmy, take Mrs Neville's bag and put it in Judith's room, please."

Soon they were all sitting together around the kitchen table having tea. Judith was keen to relate to her mother her achievements on the farm, care of the horses, cooking, and the planting of the potatoes.

"Mummy, I must get changed and then you can come to see the stable."

"The children all have some responsibilities, even Pauline helps with the egg collection," said Vera.

"How very charming," commented Veronica.

"Off you all go," said Vera.

When the children had all left, Veronica said to Vera, "You really are very kind to have taken in all these children, but, if you'll pardon me for saying so, I don't really think that this is the right environment for my daughter."

Vera carefully controlled her response and said, "How do you mean?"

"Well, surely you appreciate that Judith comes from a different sort of home than the others. I mean, she has had a different sort of upbringing."

"Veronica, I suggest that you spend a little time with Judith. I think that you will see that she has adapted well and is very happy here."

"I'm not sure that I want her to adapt to life as a farmer."

The kitchen door opened, and Judith rushed in.

"Mummy, come and see the horses. I have to feed them and give them a grooming."

"My dear, what on earth are you wearing?"

"These are my dungarees, Mrs Orton made them for me for when I'm working. I got the jodhpur boots for Christmas. Mum, I mean Mrs Orton, bought them from a neighbour. Her daughter had grown out of them."

"How generous of you, Vera. Show me the way then and let's see the horses."

"Veronica, I suggest that you borrow a pair of my boots. It can be a bit messy in the stable, though I have to say that Judith keeps it in very good order when she mucks out."

"Mucks out?"

"Come, Mummy, I'll explain."

Vera could put it off no longer. She took a deep breath and steeled herself for the conversation with Alfie and Pauline. She could not help but wonder how she had got into this situation. She was a widow, a farmer, and mother to one son.

Her life had now got so much more complicated as a result of this awful war.

Breaking such tragic news to the young children and explaining what had happened to their mother was so difficult that Vera spent a long time answering their questions and trying to comfort them.

Finally, Alfie asked, "But what's going to happen to us? Dad is on a ship somewhere."

"Yes, and it is a secret about where his ship is. I'm sure that as soon as he comes back to England, he will visit us. You've so much to tell him. And remember, you have a loving family here, you are not alone. You have a mum and a big brother and sister."

After they dried their tears, the conversation ended with an agreement that they would all go to church the next day and say a prayer for Mrs Field.

"Now, I want you both to come and help me to get supper ready. Alfie, I want you to teach Pauline to peel potatoes. Come on, let's get busy."

Some time later, while they were preparing the supper, Vera heard raised voices and quickly realised that there was an argument going on between mother and daughter. The kitchen door opened.

"I will not!"

"But, darling, it will be best for you."

"I'm staying here."

"You can stay with Granny."

"I am not going to leave my horses."

Judith rushed past Vera and ran up the stairs. There was the sound of a door slamming.

"I'm sorry about this fuss, Vera. Judith does not realise what is best for her."

Vera was on the point of saying, "Perhaps she does", when she quickly decided that it might not be a good idea.

"Perhaps she will feel differently when she has had time to think about it," said Vera.

"I really hope so, I have to work on Monday and then I am going to take Judith back to London with me on Tuesday."

"You are working here on the Island?"

"Yes. I can't tell you what my job is. Well, perhaps I can mention only that a German speaker is required for interrogation of a prisoner."

"A pilot?"

"Sorry, it's confidential. Can I help you with the meal?"

When the supper was ready, Vera managed to coax Judith to join the others, but there was no doubt that she was an unhappy girl. Later, after the kitchen was cleared, Jimmy instructed Veronica on how to light and extinguish the oil lamp in the bedroom.

"If you will excuse me, Vera, I'll get an early night. Judith, darling, do be reasonable, we'll talk about you know what in the morning."

The next day, Sunday, they all went to the tiny old church at Bonchurch. The older children walked in both directions and Vera drove Veronica. Tim just managed to get up the very steep hill from the church out of the village with only the driver and passenger.

After lunch, Vera said, "All children get changed out of your school uniforms that you wore to church. Judith and Jimmy, can you tack up the horses? Alfie, would you like to go with them to help with your pony and Daisy too?"

83

Jimmy and Judith were last to leave the kitchen and, as they did so, Jimmy said, "Can Judith and I canter today?"

Vera said in a quiet voice, "Please remember that Alfie has had very bad news, you must think of him and not only yourself. I want you to walk around the paddock with him on his pony, Sally. Remember, he is still quite a new rider."

"Are you going to ride too?" asked Judith.

"No, I shall introduce Pauline to Daisy and start her lessons. Veronica, would you like to come to watch?"

"Yes, please, Mummy!" said Judith.

"You can borrow my boots, Veronica."

Mrs Neville spent much of the afternoon watching the children riding and having fun together. She could not fail to see how her daughter's riding skills had improved and how much she was enjoying herself.

It was later, after teatime, that Vera remembered the German dictionary. Veronica had gone to her room to do some work, and the rest of them were sitting round the kitchen table.

"Judith, shall we see if you can translate more of the writing on the pilot's envelope?"

The girl was more relaxed than she had been the previous day, mainly because her mother had chosen not to discuss the matter of her leaving the farm.

TRUE FACTS

In 1940, when the British armed forces were at their weakest, after a number of military setbacks, Hitler planned to invade England in September. However, his generals persuaded him to wait until May 1941, when the German forces would be better prepared.

The invasion was code named

"Operation Sealion"

"Yes, have you got the dictionary?"

"It's on the cupboard. Bring it to the table and get the folder."

Judith had everyone's attention as she flicked through the dictionary pages.

"Let's see, *Unternehmen Seelöwe*. Here we are, *Unternehemen*. It says 'operation.'"

"And the other word, *seelöwe*?"

They were all silent, waiting for Judith to find the word.

"Sea lion!"

"Sea lion? Are you sure?" said Jimmy.

"Yes, look, there it is."

"So, the words on the front mean, 'Top Secret, Operation Sealion'! exclaimed Vera.

"What can that be? Let's look inside the envelope, Judith," said Jimmy.

He grabbed it from her and tipped it up over the table. Out fell a number of documents and maps. They started to look through them.

"Look, this map shows arrows pointing at Bournemouth Beach. It must be for an attack!"

"Let's see, Jimmy. What does that say?" said an excited Alfie, grabbing at the papers.

Vera pushed his hand away.

"Careful, careful, don't tear them, Alfie."

"It says, *Heeresgruppe C, General von Leeb*."

"Look that up, Judith."

"Wait, Jimmy, give me a chance."

Judith leafed through the dictionary pages again.

"It means 'army group.'"

"So, the map shows that Army Group C, with General von Leeb in command, is going to attack Bournemouth Beach."

"That's right, Mum. And look here, there are photos of the beach, and there, look at the typed page, it's a list of some sort."

The door opened and Veronica came in.

"What are you all doing? Some sort of game?"

"Mummy, you speak German, look at this paper."

Judith passed her mother the list.

"Where did you get this from? It's a list of tanks and guns."

"I got this black folder from the plane that landed here. The pilot was desperate to get it so that he could destroy it."

"Show me the other papers," requested Veronica abruptly. Judith passed them to her and she sat down and started leafing through all the documents. "Vera, where is the nearest telephone?"

"Well, there used to be one in the guest house. I don't know if they still have one there."

"Could you drive me there please?"

"What, now?"

"Yes, these documents are extremely important. I suppose I should tell you. We know that Hitler is planning to invade England. We had thought that the Germans would try to land on the Isle of Wight. That's why all those tanks and army lorries have been arriving here. These documents show that we were wrong. The main attack will be along the Bournemouth coast."

"Jimmy, put all the papers away in the envelope and give it and the folder to Judith's mother. Off you go to do your jobs while I take Mrs Neville to the guest house."

In the rush to get to a telephone, no one noticed at first that the smaller, unopened envelope had been left behind. When Judith saw it, she put it into the cupboard.

As they bumped along down the farm track, Vera said to her passenger, "May I assume that the real reason that you wanted Judith to leave the Island is that you feared that there would be a German invasion here?"

Veronica laughed and said, "You are very perceptive, Vera. Yes, and I am sorry if I offended you with what I said earlier. Seeing the children riding this afternoon, I couldn't fail to notice how happy they all are together. I've changed my mind and am glad for Judith to stay."

CHAPTER 10

Suspicions are Aroused

When the children came down for breakfast, they were surprised to find that Judith's mother was already there drinking tea with Mum.

"Well, children, Mrs Neville has to leave us earlier than we had expected."

"Yes, I can tell you children that the papers you gave me really are very important. So important in fact that I have orders to take them to London today. An army car is coming to pick me up soon."

"Must you really go already, Mummy?" asked Judith.

"I'm afraid so, darling. Judith, let's go to your room for a little talk."

"But I am in a hurry for school."

"You have a few minutes to spare, Judith, it will be quicker to get to school today. You are not going by tractor but in Tim."

"And it's downhill all the way!" quipped Jimmy.

When mother and daughter returned to the kitchen, Judith was smiling from ear to ear.

"Good news, Judith?" asked Vera knowingly.

"Very good news, Mum. I am going to stay, that is if you will let me!"

"What do you think, children, shall we let her stay?"

"Yes!" shouted Alfie.

"Well, I suppose so," said Jimmy.

Judith aimed a pretend punch at him, and he ducked, laughing.

"Vera, I have given Judith a telephone number where she can contact me day or night, should there be any problems. I know you don't have a phone, but I will arrange with the commander of the prison camp for you to use theirs, should the need arise."

There was great enthusiasm among the children to restart their school, an enthusiasm that overcame Judith's sadness at the early departure of her mother. This keenness was not because they longed to get back to lessons, but for two other reasons. Firstly, they would arrive at the school gate by car! They would be the only children who did not walk to school or come by bike or bus. The other cause for excitement was that they had an extraordinary tale to tell about a German plane landing in the field where they were working and that they had actually met the pilot!

Vera dropped the older children off and then drove to the primary school with Alfie and Pauline before driving back to the farm to check on the work the Italians were doing. And so, after the excitement of the previous week, life on the farm settled back into an established routine, though things were changing for the prisoners of war. The two English soldiers had become much more relaxed. No longer did they have bayonets fixed on their rifles, and now there was less suspicion and mistrust between the prisoners and the guards. It was clear too that, apart from Luigi, the Italians worked hard and were clearly very useful around the farm.

It was Saturday morning, while Jimmy was cleaning his room, that he found a folded, somewhat crumpled piece of paper. It was the one Private Jenkins had given him on the day he climbed into the cockpit of the aircraft. There was a clear imprint of the soldier's muddy boot on one edge. Jimmy unfolded the paper. One side was printed with a list of things. At the top in big letters it said, La Taverne de Le Havre. On the other side, there were some handwritten notes in a foreign language and a sketch map of the Isle of Wight.

"Judith! Judith!" shouted Jimmy.

A voice from downstairs called, "She's busy, Jimmy. What do you want?"

"I want to show her a paper the pilot dropped."

"You'll have to wait until she's finished the sweeping. Hurry up with your room, you've got the carpets to beat."

The boy realised that there was no point in arguing, and he hurried to finish his room.

It was somewhat later, as Jimmy was carrying the carpets back indoors, that he saw Judith.

"What was it you wanted to show me?" she asked.

Jimmy put the carpet he was holding back in its normal place and then pushed his hand into his pocket and withdrew the crumpled paper. He gave it to Judith and said, "Here, look at this while I get the last carpet in."

Judith uncrumpled the paper and gave a whoop as she read it.

"This is a menu! It's from a French restaurant in Le Havre. How did you get it?"

"Private Jenkins gave it to me. He found it by the plane on the day it landed."

"Why didn't you tell us?"

"Well, I forgot about it."

"Let's have a look," exclaimed Alfie, reaching for the paper.

"Careful, Alfie, don't tear it."

As Judith pulled it away from him, he could see the back of the menu.

"Look, there's some stuff on the back," he said.

"Yes, there's some writing in another language and some numbers," stated Jimmy.

"Children, why don't you put it on the table so we can all see it?" urged Vera.

She cleared away a few things, and Judith placed the paper on the table with the menu upwards.

"So, what do we learn from this?" asked Vera.

"Well, it tells us one thing," said Judith.

"What's that?" asked Alfie.

"Where Hans had flown from, Le Havre. You see the date on the menu is 24th Février. That's February in French, and it's the day before he landed here."

"He didn't tell us where he flew from, did he?" said Vera.

"What about the other side of the paper?" asked Alfie.

Judith turned the paper over.

"What language is that, Judith?" asked Jimmy.

"It's German, but the handwriting is very bad. It's difficult to read."

"Look there's a map of the Isle of Wight!" exclaimed Alfie.

"Well, I wouldn't call it a map, it's a rough diagram. But look – Ventnor is written by the side of it, with an arrow pointing to near here."

"But why would the pilot mark this place, Judith?" asked Vera.

"What do the German language say there?" queried Alfie, as he pushed a finger at the map.

"Careful, Alfie! Mum, do you still have the dictionary we borrowed from the library?"

"Yes, it's in the cupboard where the black folder was. Oh gosh, be careful, the pistol is still there!"

"I'll get it for you," said Jimmy.

"Look, children, let's give Judith some minutes to look up the words she doesn't know while we get lunch ready. You go up to your room and get some peace and quiet, Judith."

As Jimmy gave Judith the dictionary, he said, "We forgot to give Mrs Neville the other envelope."

"Which envelope?" asked Vera.

"The one with his family photos, I suppose."

"Can't we look at them, Mum? It would be fun to see what his family look like."

"All right, but after lunch. I must remember tomorrow to talk to the corporal about getting the envelope sent to Hans, wherever they have taken him."

Over lunch there was much discussion about why the German had drawn a diagram of the Isle of Wight and marked the position of Ventnor. It was only after they had cleared away and washed up that they once more crowded around the paper on the table. With a flourish, Judith placed a second sheet of paper beside the first; on it was her neat handwriting.

"Quiet, everyone. Now this is my translation of his awful handwriting. She pointed to a line on the back of the menu.

"That line says, 'Le Havre to Ventnor distance 160 kilometres.' The next line says, 'Petrol needed for flight distance 160 kms = 80 litres'."

"Is that all it says?" asked Alfie.

"Not quite, there are two words underneath, which mean, 'Wind southwest'."

"Well, it all means nothing to me," said Vera. "Let's look at the photos."

"No, wait a minute. The writing must be important in some way."

"But in what way, Jimmy?" asked Judith.

"I don't know, I'll have to think about it."

Vera pulled open the flap of the brown envelope and pulled out the contents, two photos. She laid them side by side on the table. The children clamoured to look over her shoulder.

Judith pointed to one with a single person on it and said, "That must be his wife, she looks very nice, but quite serious."

"She is very well dressed, and such beautiful black hair. What does it say on the bottom of the photo, Judith? The handwriting," added Vera.

"Um, *Zu Hans mit Liebe.* That means, 'To Hans with love,'" said Judith.

"Let's have a look at the children," said Jimmy.

Vera lifted the photo from the table and showed everyone, saying, "They are with their mother in this picture, two young boys."

"Yes, with black hair, like her. But that's very peculiar."

"What d'ya mean, Judith?" asked Alfie.

"I distinctly remember Hans saying to me that he had two children and their hair was the same colour as mine."

"That's true, Mum. But didn't he also say that he had a boy about Judith's age and a little girl!?" exclaimed Jimmy.

There was silence round the table while they contemplated the contradictions.

It was Alfie who spoke first. "He never told us the truth, did he?"

"You should always tell the truth," added Pauline.

"That's right, Pauline," said Vera.

"But why would he lie to us?" asked Judith.

"Perhaps these are the wrong pictures, he got them mixed up with someone else's," said Jimmy.

"No, that can't be so because on one of them it says, 'To Hans with Love,'" Judith pointed out.

"It's all very mysterious. Firstly, we have the note on the back of the menu. Why would he have a map of the Island and Ventnor marked on it?" asked Vera.

"And secondly, on that piece of paper he had calculated how much fuel he needed to get just to here. Besides, he told us he was attacked by a Spitfire and had to land here because his petrol tank was hit."

"That's true, Jimmy. And thirdly, the photos. It's almost as if he had never seen the picture of the children because they certainly don't look like his description to us!" exclaimed Judith excitedly.

Vera raised her hand to quell the general hubbub and said, "Do you know, there is a fourth thing."

"What fourth thing?" asked Alfie.

"The fuss he made when I tried to persuade him to let me dress the wound on his arm. We never saw that wound. I wonder if it existed."

"But his jacket was ripped, there was a hole and it looked like there were blood there," said Alfie.

"Yes, it was ripped, and it looked like blood, but was it really blood?"

"That's right, Mum, and that reminds me, there's a fifth thing! When I sat in the cockpit of the plane, I looked all around, and I couldn't see bullet holes anywhere."

"But they was on the outside of the plane," said Alfie.

"True, but he was on the inside."

"Come on, we've got work to do. Put the photos away. I don't suppose we shall ever know the answer to all these things. We would need a detective to find out the truth."

There was a short silence before Judith and Jimmy shouted simultaneously, "We have one!"

"Who?" asked Alfie.

"Yes, Luigi, the major!" exclaimed Vera.

CHAPTER 11

Major Balzarini the Detective

"But how can we talk to Luigi, he's in the prisoner of war camp at the weekend and during the week when he is working here, we are at school," said Jimmy.

"Yeah, we don't see him and the others, no more," added Alfie.

"Well, I could talk to him during the week, but it's your mystery, so it would be best if you could tell him about it," said Vera.

"But how?" asked Judith.

"I know. I thought that you could all have a ride tomorrow. I'll walk beside Daisy while Pauline has her first ride. We could go past the old guest house, where the prisoners are, and ask if we could speak with Luigi."

"Yes! That would be good."

Early on Saturday afternoon, when all the chores had been done, the procession of four riders and Vera on foot, closed the farm gate and turned right in the direction of the guest house.

"Look, there are some army tents pitched in the garden," called Jimmy, who was on the tallest horse and could see over the high hedge.

"I expect they are for the soldiers who are stationed here to guard the prisoners of war," said Vera. "Slow down, Jimmy, I'll go to talk with those two sentries."

The two men were surprised by the unexpected sight in front of them.

"Can we help you, Ma'am?" said one.

"Hello, yes, I wonder if you could arrange for me to speak with Major Balzarini?"

The soldiers looked at each other and grinned.

The man who had spoken earlier turned to Vera and in an unfriendly fashion said, "This is not a hotel, Ma'am, it's a prisoner of war camp. No one goes in or out without an officer's permission."

The soldier had underestimated Vera, for she was not to be deterred.

"Then could I speak to Captain Morley, please?"

The two men looked at each other again and one mumbled something to the other.

"Is he a friend of yours, Ma'am?"

Vera decided that in this situation, the truth could be stretched a bit.

"Yes, please inform him that Mrs Orton would like to see him."

"Hang on, Ma'am, I'll speak to the officer of the watch."

The soldier picked up his rifle, which had been standing on the ground in front of him, put it on his shoulder, turned, and marched to the front door of the big house. He banged on the door, it was opened, and he disappeared inside.

Vera and the children waited, though the horses were getting increasingly impatient to continue their exercise.

"Jimmy, you, Judith, and Alfie walk on to the green, and I'll catch up with you as soon as I can. No cantering until I get there!"

The riders had time to trot up and down the green area three times before their mum arrived with Pauline sitting on Daisy.

"The major is coming for tea with Corporal Trent at half past three!" Vera called out to the children. "Alfie, you come and walk with me and Pauline. Judith and Jimmy, you can canter up and down the green if you want to. Judith, do you have your watch on? We must leave here at half past two so that we can get the horses put away before our guests arrive."

It was a rush, but by three thirty, the whole family were sitting expectantly around the kitchen table waiting for their visitors.

"Let's hope they are a bit late," said Vera. "The kettle hasn't boiled yet."

Billy, barking at the front door, announced the arrival of the major and his escort. Vera went to welcome them.

There was no mistaking Luigi's voice as he was guided into the kitchen by Vera.

"Signora Vera, I am most honoured by your kind invitation to celebrate the most famous English teatime with you and your family."

"The pleasure is ours, Luigi. Do sit down over there. Corporal, you are welcome to join us at the table or you can sit in the armchair by the stove."

"I'll take the armchair, if you please, Ma'am. It's a joy to get some warmth. Them tents lack such home comforts. By the way, the captain asked me to tell you that the road will be very noisy later today. There will be a big troop movement of soldiers from around Ventnor leaving the Island, mobile guns and tanks too. They are waiting for darkness to avoid enemy planes."

"Thank you for warning us, Corporal."

The soldier propped his rifle against the wall and sat down. It was not long before he was dozing.

As soon as the tea had been poured and some pleasantries exchanged, Vera, recognising the children's impatience, introduced the subject they wanted raised.

"Luigi, when we first met, you told us that before you were a soldier, you were a detective."

"This is indeed true, Signora, a detective of some rank."

"Well, since you are here, I wonder if you can use your skills to help solve a mystery."

"A mystery! Please tell me about it. I am most keen to assist in finding a solution."

"Well, it is really the children's mystery. I'll let them tell you about it. Alfie, you start. Tell the major about the pilot and his bad arm."

"It were me who saw him first. He never scared me, I just stood still when he jumped down from the wing. He gave me his pistol."

"But tell the major about the pilot's arm," insisted Vera.

"Oh yea, he had a hole in his jacket and there were blood round it. He couldn't hold anything."

"And tell me, young man, did he say what had happened to his arm?" asked the major.

"He said he had been shot by a Spitfire, but only a bit."

"Only a bit? Is that what he said?"

"No sir, he said 'slightly'."

Jimmy interrupted and said, "Later, when I went into the cockpit, I couldn't see any holes."

"No damage at all?"

"No, sir, none."

"And, Signora, did you see this injury he had received?"

"No, he refused to let me put a bandage on it. He went to the lavatory and put a plaster on to it himself."

"Very strange, for I can tell you from my unfortunate experience in North Africa, that the machine gun of your Spitfire is very damaging indeed."

The children, occasionally prompted by Vera, went through all the other reasons that raised their suspicions about the pilot. It was when Judith mentioned that her mother had rushed off to London, because of the importance of the documents, that Luigi suddenly threw his head back, slapped the table with his open hands and uttered loudly, "Mamma Mia, brilliant!"

The others round the table stared at the major, shocked by his loud outburst. Even the corporal stirred in his slumber.

"What's brilliant?" asked Jimmy.

"What do you mean?" questioned Vera.

"The whole idea was brilliant, a work of genius, but, but my dear friends, there were in the planning some, how do you say, 'Up slips'.

"You mean 'slip ups,'" corrected Judith.

"Yes, that is what I mean, dear friends. Terrible slip ups."

The major contorted his face into a severe grimace. He looked around the table and stared into the eyes of each onlooker in turn as he prepared himself for a dramatic statement. There was almost absolute silence; the only source of noise was the purr of the dozing soldier in the armchair.

"*Amici*,[9] my fondness for you all is very strong, but it is with the deepest of regret that I cannot tell you the solution to this mystery."

There was shock around the table and several utterances asking, "Why not?"

The major waited for silence, and then, once more, went through the facial contortions before speaking slowly and seriously.

"War has brought us together and our friendship has blossomed like flowers in spring, and it is equally beautiful. But I am a soldier in an army which is in conflict with your own. Although I am a prisoner, I must, for my conscience, be loyal to my country and my men. It is therefore impossible for me to tell you the solution to your mystery and satisfy your quest."

There was shocked silence in the room. After some seconds, Vera spoke up.

"Well, Luigi, we are very disappointed, especially after the comments you made about something being brilliant. This made us even more curious! However, we must respect what you say about your loyalty."

"Thank you, Signora Vera. However, I am resolved not to disappoint you totally. No, some satisfaction must be awarded. Therefore, I propose to explain what led me to solve the treacherous mystery, but…but I will leave you to make the conclusion yourselves."

---

9   Amici - Friends

The mood in the room brightened and there were some smiles.

"Before I begin, may I ask la Signora if I might have another piece of the most excellent cake you have baked."

CHAPTER 12

Treachery Exposed

"My friends, let me begin at the beginning. No, I will let you begin at the beginning. What is the oldest clue?"

"The pilot's wounded arm," exclaimed Alfie.

"No, it is from some time before you met the pilot, young man."

"The paper, the one the soldier gave Jimmy!" said Judith triumphantly.

"Yes, and this was the first of several most terrible slip ups. The pilot should have destroyed this paper before he even took off, for this shows in a precise way how he planned his flight, where he was going, and most importantly exactly how much fuel he would need to arrive at his destination with an empty fuel tank."

"But he said that the Spitfire shot a hole in his tank!" exclaimed Alfie.

"Young Alfie, I regret to be the carrier of disappointment to you, but there was no attack by a Spitfire."

"But how can you know?" asked a perplexed Jimmy.

"While we were working in the field of potatoes, one of my men, Salvatore, the engineer, was quite overcome with interest in the plane. He inspected the damage made by the bullets and found a situation most peculiar. There were bullet holes in the side of the plane but no bullets! There would most certainly have been bullets inside the metal. His conclusion was that the holes were made not by bullets, but by a sharp metal tool."

"But the petrol tank!" shouted Jimmy.

"Ah yes, this was another slip up, for although the tank may have been empty, any engineer would have found that there were no holes in it."

"So, if there was no shooting, then how did he hurt his arm?" asked Alfie.

"He didn't. As part of the treachery a hole had been made in his jacket and some red fluid painted round it. Another slip up, for la Signora almost discovered the truth when she tried to cover the supposed wound."

While the major stopped to take a bite of his cake, all eyes, (except Corporal Trent's), were upon him. He carefully wiped his mouth with his handkerchief, clearly savouring not only the cake, but also the tension he had built up in the room.

He looked around the table and then said, "As an honest man, even I, a professional detective, have to admit that I am perplexed about why *Oberleutnant* Hans Seitz, asked Jimmy to recover the documents. Tell me, do you recall the conversation you had with the pilot before he suddenly exclaimed, "Donner und Blitzen" and asked Jimmy to try to find the black folder?"

Judith, without hesitation, said, "I remember Mum said that his appearance had made a lot of excitement around here."

"That's right, Mum, and I told him that there were people wanting to get souvenirs from the plane."

There was a pause, before Luigi said slowly and with great emphasis, "Ah ha, then I have the answer to that which has teased my brain."

"What is the reason then, please do tell us," pleaded Vera.

"If I answer your enthusiastic request, it will give you the biggest and most clear clue to this whole mystery. I will do so, but my loyalty to my country permits me to say no more. So please respect this."

The listeners were on the edge of their seats.

"Yes, of course Luigi, we can understand your situation," said Vera.

He started to speak very slowly and precisely, to embellish the drama. "When young Jimmy mentioned that souvenir hunters might steal from the plane, the pilot suddenly realised that the object of his whole mission might not be found by a military search but could fall into the hands of those who waited to plunder the aircraft – souvenir hunters."

"Object? You mean the folder?" asked Judith.

"My dear Judith, as I have said, I will not answer any further questions, but I must complement you for your intelligence."

The others round the table looked at each other and smiled, while Vera held her forefinger to her lips to indicate silence.

Luigi continued, "The pilot had realised that there was a much better chance that the 'object' would come to the attention of the army authorities if it found its way into your hands. As for the photos, it was never intended that you should see them and it is obvious that he had never either.

The German intelligence had made up the story of his family but made the most horrible slip up by not giving him good information about them."

"But why did they make up the story of his family?" asked Vera.

"The Germans must have thought that it was more likely that the British would have believed a story told by an officer. So, they made an ordinary pilot falsely into a high-ranking officer, gave him a name, a rank and a family."

"So, his name is not Hans?"

"Probably not."

There was a long silence, which was at last broken by Luigi saying softly, "It was a brilliant idea, but the planners were very careless. It is getting dark, now I must return to my men and tomorrow we will return to work for you. I thank you, dear Signora Vera for your most generous hospitality."

As soon as Vera returned to the kitchen after seeing the major to the door with a sleepy corporal, the chattering started.

"Stop, everyone, don't all speak at once! Let's consider the evidence the major has explained to us."

"Mum, I know the answer!!"

"Wait, Judith, let's discuss it together. Now what about the pilot?"

The three older children put up their hands, just as they would at school, but Pauline had a different idea and blurted out, "He don't tell the truth."

"That's right, Pauline. So, what do you think, Judith?"

"That's just what this is about: the truth. Hans the pilot lied to us, but I think that there was a much bigger lie!"

Jimmy could resist no longer. "That's right! It's the document, that's the big lie!"

"Why do you think that, Jimmy?"

"Well, Mum, he flew directly to Ventnor and ran out of petrol, so he was bound to be caught with the documents, but that was the whole idea. This treachery was disguised by pretending that he had been shot at and had to land."

Judith interrupted, "The Germans wanted our army to believe that the invasion would land at Bournemouth."

"And so our soldiers would be in the wrong place when the enemy landed!" shouted Alfie.

"That's exactly what I think!" said Vera.

"So, what are we going to do about it?" asked Jimmy.

"What do you mean?" asked Vera.

"Well, Corporal Trent told us that the army is moving out from Ventnor tonight!"

"Gosh you are right, Jimmy!"

"We got to stop them," urged Alfie.

They all rushed out of the front door. In the distance they could hear the tramp of soldiers marching and the groan of heavy vehicles straining to get up the steep hill out of the town.

"Run in and get your coats on. Pauline, you stay here and watch out of the window. Jimmy, you run to the prisoner of war camp and demand to see Captain Morley. Explain that we are trying to stop the troops leaving and why. Tell him he must come and help. Judith, Alfie jump in Tim."

Vera started up the little car and raced along the bumpy farm track with the two children being thrown about in the back. When they reached the gate, Alfie jumped out and opened it. Vera rushed through and turned Tim towards where the army was advancing. She could see the dim illumination of the first tank's headlights as it rumbled towards her. She parked in the middle of the road and put the hand brake on. Tim was blocking the tank's path.

"Get out quickly, Judith! Alfie, stay away!"

Just as they got back to the gate there was a bang and the sound of crunching metal and glass. The first tank stopped, and several soldiers ran forward to see what had happened. By the men's torches, Vera and the others could see the mangled mass of aluminium and steel that had once been Tim. The soldiers started to pick up pieces and throw them into the ditch at the side of the road.

"There's no one in the car, Sergeant," called a soldier.

"Clear as much as you can then the tanks can flatten the rest."

Vera and the children were quite unseen in the darkness at the side of the road.

"We have to use our secret weapon! Judith, Alfie, open the gate to the pasture and find your way round the back of the herd. They always spend the night by the water trough. Clap your hands and shout, the cows will come out through the gate, and I'll guide them on to the road."

There was the clang of bits of metal banging against each other as the soldiers worked, but after what seemed an age, another sound filled the air: that of a herd of beef cows who were angry at being disturbed. Soon the road in front of the military transport was filled with the mooing animals.

Vera decided that the time had come for her to betray her whereabouts. She strode up to the men with torches and shouted, "Where is the officer in charge?"

One of the men shone his torch at Vera.

"Where did you come from?" said the soldier.

Another said, "This your car?"

"Yes, it is, and see what you have done to it! I want to speak to your officer."

"What's going on here, Sergeant?" said voice in the dark, which belonged to a man just coming from behind the tank.

"It's the lady here, sir. Her car has had an accident."

Someone from above them, obviously one of the tank crew, shouted, "She parked it in the middle of the road with no lights on."

"Is this true, madam?"

"Yes, it is. I want to stop you leaving Ventnor!"

"I beg your pardon?"

"I have information about a German plot to fool you all. I had to stop you."

There was some laughter among the soldiers.

"Silence, men, clear up the wreckage and continue. You, madam, are creating a serious offence in trying to hinder our progress."

Before Vera could answer, the voice from above them on the tank shouted, "Beg pardon, sir, but we can't, the road ahead is full of cows."

The animals had discovered the fresh greenery on both sides of the road and were enjoying a late meal.

The officer was furious.

"Whose cows are these, madam?" he demanded.

"Mine."

"Then for heaven's sake get them off the road!"

"No."

There was absolute silence apart from the purring of the tank engine. The men were waiting to see what the officer would do next.

"You men, you with the torches, remove the cows! You, madam, will be reported to the police and the military authorities, you will be dealt with severely."

Just as he finished speaking, there was the increasingly loud sound of a vehicle approaching from the direction the army were heading. Several torches were pointed towards it, and they all watched as a motorbike and side car weaved in and out of the cows. It stopped by the remains of Tim, and a man jumped out of the side car.

"Who is in charge here?" shouted Captain Morley as he walked towards the torches.

"Me, Lieutenant Greyson."

"I'm Captain Morley, would you be good enough to halt your transport column and await new orders."

"Yes, sir. Sergeant, tell the marching men to stand down and await orders and all the vehicles to stop engines. May I ask the reason for this delay?"

"You may, Lieutenant, but I cannot tell you, the matter is top secret. Are you all right, Mrs Orton?"

"Yes, but my car isn't. Come on, children, we have a herd of cows to recover."

<hr/>

Much later, nursing their cups of cocoa, the inhabitants of Cliff Top Farm all sat round the kitchen table discussing their exciting evening.

"What happened when you got to the prison camp, Jimmy?" asked Vera.

"Well, fortunately for me, Private Jenkins was on guard duty. He recognised me and understood that it must be an important matter. He took me in to see the captain."

"What did you tell him, Jimmy?"

"Judith, your real mum must be important because when I quickly told him of our suspicions, he phoned her, she had given him her number in case you needed to contact her. I told her what we had discovered about the pilot. Then she spoke to the captain, to ask him to delay the convoy."

"What a team we are! Well done everyone. However, the bad news is that you will all have to ride to school on the tractor trailer tomorrow!"

"Poor Tim!" said Judith.

"And the good news is that Captain Morley feels sure that the army will replace the car for us."

"We'll call it Tim Two!" suggested Alfie, and everyone agreed.

Later, when the children had gone to bed, Vera watched out of the window. At the end of the farm track, she could see the dim lights of the vehicles being turned round and beginning the journey back to where they had started.

The invasion of England never came. Hitler changed his mind. Vera always wondered if in uncovering the treacherous plot, the children of Cliff Top Farm had some tiny part in influencing him.

TRUE FACTS

One morning in October 1940, nineteen-year-old, Harold Blow was driving a lorry along a country road on the Isle of Wight. Suddenly, a man wearing an airman's uniform stepped into the road. It was a German pilot in full flying gear. *Feldwebel* (Sergeant) Horst Hellriegel had been in a battle with British aircraft over the Dorset coast when his fuel tanks were riddled with bullets.

With no way of reaching his French base, he had landed his Messerschmitt 109 on a nearby hill and then walked to the road.

Harold asked the German if he was armed, but the man said no. Nevertheless, Harold searched him before allowing him into his lorry. They drove to the village of Carisbrooke and to the local policeman's house. However, the policeman was away on holiday. Not knowing what to do with the pilot, Harold drove to his mother's house, where she was preparing lunch.

Later, the local newspaper interviewed Mrs Blow. Here is what she said:

"I wasn't frightened of him. I fancy he was a little frightened of me as he kept on saying that he was not a bomber and trembled like a leaf.

"He showed me a photo of his wife and little daughter and said he did not want to fight England. I said, 'Then why do your people come over here dropping bombs on women and children?'

"He shook his head sadly and said 'I know. It is terrible. It is very bad for our women and children too.'

"I gave him a cup of tea and a plate of meat, and he took some toffees out of his pocket and gave them to my little girl. Harold went for the police, and after about half an hour they arrived with eight soldiers, and two of them came into the kitchen. I said, 'There's no need for that — the man has already surrendered, and you must wait outside until he's finished his cup of tea!'"

The abandoned Messerschmitt sat on the hill, guarded for the first few days, after which the locals arrived with tools to plunder the plane. Some were later prosecuted in court.

The local newspaper reported, "Portions of a Messerschmitt 109, ranging from an electrical generator to an engine cover three feet long, were exhibited in Court when seven souvenir hunters were charged with removing parts of a German aeroplane."

Horst spent the rest of the war in a prisoner of war camp.

Making *Tagliatelle*
by hand

Ideally, the flour that should be used to make *tagliatelle* is called 00 flour. However, Vera only had normal flour, which is not as fine. Nevertheless, normal flour will do, though the *tagliatell*e will not be as soft.

This recipe will make enough for two to three people. It takes about an hour to prepare and three to four minutes to cook.

Ingredients

- 200g flour
- 2 large eggs
- A pinch of salt

Tools

- Rolling pin
- Fork

- Wooden board
- Pasta cutter or knife

Step 1 Making the dough

- On a clean work surface, make a mound of the flour. Save a little flour to use later.
- Make a hole in the centre of the mound big enough to hold the contents of the two eggs.
- Crack the two eggs into the hole.
- Beat the egg mixture with the fork, slowly pulling the flour from the sides of the hole until the egg has all been absorbed by the flour. As the mixture thickens, use your hands to mix the flour and eggs.
- If necessary, add a little warm water and continue mixing until the flour is formed into a ball of dough.

Step 2 Kneading the Dough

- Clean the work surface of flour and small bits of dough and then spread some flour on it.
- Knead the dough by pressing the heel of one hand into the ball, keeping fingers high.
- Turn the dough over, then use knuckles to press into the dough, one hand at a time. This process should be carried out around 10 times.
- Roll the dough back into a ball and repeat the stretching and knuckling process, using more flour if needed to prevent any stickiness.
- Repeat the process for about 10-20 minutes until the dough is smooth and silky.

- Roll the dough into a smooth ball.

Step 3 Resting the dough

- Place the dough in a small bowl and cover with a cloth or cling film.
- Let the dough rest for at least 30 minutes.

Step 4 Rolling the Pasta

- Spread flour lightly on the work surface.
- Make the dough into the shape of a circle.
- With a rolling pin, begin rolling the dough, starting in the centre and rolling to the outer edge.
- Turn the dough a quarter-turn, and repeat, working round, until the sheet of dough is 3mm thin or less. Scatter a small amount of flour on the dough whenever it starts to stick to the surface of the rolling pin. It is very important to make the dough as thin as possible.
- According to Italian tradition, the sheet of dough should be transparent enough to read a newspaper text beneath!

Step 5 Cutting the pasta

- Place the dough onto a clean and lightly floured work surface. Roll it over itself a few times carefully, ensuring there is enough flour so it does not stick. Trim the end edges to be even, then cut it into approximately 6mm-wide strips.

- Carefully lift the pasta strips and place them gently onto a tea towel, making sure that they are separated.
- Repeat this with any remaining sheets of dough.

Step 6 Cooking the pasta

- Boil a large pot of water. When it is boiling add several pinches of salt.
- Gently put the pasta into the water and boil for 3 to 4 minutes.
- Strain the pasta and mix with a sauce of your choice.

Inspired by the Pasta Evangelists

Enjoy your meal!
Buon appetito!
Bon appetit!
Guten Appetit!

ACKNOWLEDGEMENTS

I have always wanted to write some stories set in the period of the second war, the time when I was born. However, I needed to ensure that stories about that tumultuous epoch would be of interest to children. I was fortunate enough to gather a little team of beta readers, all aged eleven to twelve, who read the first manuscript and gave me invaluable feedback. So, thank you Freja Davies, Mia Thatcher, Molly Ewen and Jessica Ewen for your help.

Thanks too to my editor, Lisl Scully, for her careful and insightful work.

As ever, thanks to my wife Barbro who provided support, encouragement and often, inspiration.

ABOUT THE AUTHOR

Michael E Wills was born on the Isle of Wight, UK, during the Second World War. He was educated at Carisbrooke Grammar and St Peter's College, Birmingham. After a long career in education, as a teacher, a teacher trainer and textbook writer, in retirement he  took up writing historical novels. His first book, *Finn's Fate*, was followed by a sequel novel, *Three Kings – One Throne*. In 2015, he started on a quartet of Viking stories for young readers called, *Children of the Chieftain*. The first book, *Betrayed*, was described by the Historical Novel Society reviewer as "An absolutely excellent novel which I could not put down" and long-listed for the Historical Novel Society 2016 Indie Prize. The second book in the quartet, *Banished*, was published in December 2015 followed in 2017 by the third book, *Bounty*. *Bound For Home* completed the series in 2019. His book for younger children, Sven and the Purse of Silver, won bronze medal in the Wishing Shelf Book Awards. Moving into a completely different and much older time period, Michael's book "Izar, The Amesbury Archer", is based in the Late Stone

Age. It won a Coffee Pot Book Club's Historical Fiction "Book of the Year" prize in 2021.

Though a lot of his spare time is spent with grandchildren, he also has a wide range of interests including researching for future books, writing, playing the guitar, carpentry and electronics.

You can find out more about Michael E Wills and the books he has written by visiting his website: www.michaelwills. eu